A GOLDEN AGE

Visions of Fantasy

AUSTRALIA'S FANTASY ILLUSTRATORS: THEIR LIVES AND WORKS

A GOLDEN AGE

Visions of Fantasy

AUSTRALIA'S FANTASY ILLUSTRATORS: THEIR LIVES AND WORKS

ROBERT HOLDEN

Angus&Robertson
An imprint of HarperCollins*Publishers*

To Ingrid and Nicholas Holden in appreciation of the golden hours they have given me and for their patience and constant support. They have heard more about May Gibbs, Ida Rentoul Outhwaite, et al. than they ever wanted to know!

AN ANGUS & ROBERTSON BOOK
An imprint of HarperCollinsPublishers

First published in Australia in 1992
by CollinsAngus&Robertson Publishers Pty Limited (ACN 009 913 517)
A division of HarperCollinsPublishers (Australia) Pty Limited
25 Ryde Road, Pymble NSW 2073, Australia

HarperCollinsPublishers (New Zealand) Limited
31 View Road, Glenfield, Auckland 10, New Zealand

HarperCollinsPublishers Limited
77– 85 Fulham Palace Road, London W6 8JB, United Kingdom

National Library of Australia
Cataloguing-in-Publication data:

Holden, Robert. .
A golden age: a treasury of Australian fantasy.
Bibliography.
Includes index.
ISBN: 0 207 17817 8.
0 207 16697 8 (v.I)
0 207 17723 6.(v.II)
1.Illustrators - Australia. 2. Illustrated books, Children's - Australia. I. Title.
741.6420922

Design based on concept from Robert Holden.
Cover: Illustration by May Gibbs that appeared on cover of the Sydney Mail, *29 April 1914.*
Printed in Singapore

5 4 3 2 1
96 95 94 93 92

Acknowledgements

I would respectfully like to acknowledge my debt to Marcie Muir's pioneering work and research and to her personal encouragement and friendship which are much valued.

Pam Brewster was the enthusiastic initiator of *A Golden Age* and her trust and belief have been appreciated.

Among other staff members of Collins/Angus & Robertson, I would like to acknowledge Claire Craig's contribution as a painstaking and thought-provoking editor.

The publishers would like to thank the following copyright holders:

Peter Badgery
DOROTHY WALL

Vaughan Evans
PIXIE O'HARRIS

Jane Glad
NORMAN LINDSAY

Peter. Lindsay
LIONEL LINDSAY

Peter H. Lindsay
PERCY LINDSAY

Alan Maltby
PEG MALTBY

Lady Martin
IDA RENTOUL OUTHWAITE

Kay & James Overton
ETHEL JACKSON MORRIS

Clytie Pate
CHRISTIAN YANDELL

Tom Quirk
ETHEL SPOWERS

Laurence & Jean Rentoul
ANNIE RENTOUL

The Spastic Centre of NSW and The NSW Society for Crippled Children
MAY GIBBS

Margaret Stanfield née Clark
MARGARET CLARK

April Hersey
ZORA CROSS

Every effort has been made to contact the owners of copyright. The publishers would welcome any further information regarding holders of copyright not mentioned above.

C o n t e n t s

MARY, MARY, QUITE CONTRARY,
HOW DOES YOUR GARDEN GROW;
SILVER BELLS AND COCKLE SHELLS
AND PRETTY MAIDS ALL IN A ROW

THIS IS THE WAY WE WASH OUR HANDS

Contents

'The Little Witch' by Ida Rentoul Outhwaite from ELVES & FAIRIES*, Melbourne, 1916.*

Introduction

Elves & Fairies versus Bib & Bub

From the 1900s to the 1940s a discernible school of fantasy illustrators in Australia created a golden age of children's book illustration. Whether it was Ida Rentoul Outhwaite's fairyland, without a threat to its gossamer-winged beauties, or May Gibbs' starker bushland fantasy, these images have become part of the pictorial vocabulary of Australia. Today, their evocative charm and genius are being reassessed and treasured. This anthology of fantasy illustration presents numerous favourites together with lesser-known works.

The enduring masterpieces of Australian children's book illustration are fantasy works. Due to technical limitations within the Australian printing trade early in the twentieth century, these masterpieces were mainly pen and ink or monochrome works. However, through the illustrative genius of D. H. Souter, Ida Rentoul Outhwaite, Norman Lindsay and May Gibbs, these limitations became a challenge rather than a burden. The graphic work of this first generation of prominent Australian children's book illustrators maintains its effect and appeal even in the face of colour printing and the more sophisticated processes of today.

In 1888, the year Ida Rentoul was born, Australia was described as a place 'where people are slow to adopt new methods' in terms of printing techniques. [1] Thirty years later, Outhwaite became one of the first to take full advantage of the eventual application of 'new methods' in her book *Elves & Fairies.* This 1916 publication is still the most sumptuous showcase of fantasy talent in Australian children's books and it is also, significantly, one of the very earliest Australian printings to utilise the three colour process. Without such printing advances, neither the pin-prick details of her pen and ink work nor the gentle range of her watercolours could have been reproduced.

The first local book produced for Australian children to contain illustrations, 1857.

This first generation of Australian children's book illustrators also had to contend with the lack of classic local texts to inspire and tempt them. All Australia's memorable fantasy illustrators were therefore compelled to embrace the role of author as well. This trend was initiated by Ida Rentoul Outhwaite who went as far as to provide finished illustrations first, in advance of any text at all!

This anthology presents Australia's fantasy illustrators in their dual capacities. In this way the mutually supportive roles of illustrator and author can be recognised and valued.

Children's book publishing, like most publishing in nineteenth-century Australia, was a sporadic and subsidiary activity, largely initiated by printers and booksellers. Given the superior quality of imported printings, the small buying public locally and our dearth of children's authors and illustrators, it is easy to appreciate why, of the 50 or so children's books published in nineteenth-century Australia, most had the appearance of frontier printings. Crude presentation using newspaper type and lack of quality generally in the writing and illustrating were the order of the day. Such works were often vanity publications issued at the author's expense or works printed to capitalise on the Christmas market (the rest of the year being a bleak wasteland of publishing inactivity).

The first two milestones in the history of Australian children's books set the tone for much of the nineteenth century. Australia's first children's book, *A Mother's Offering* (1841) by Charlotte Barton reaffirmed the role of parental care and home education in the colonies. It maintained a certain eighteenth-century attitude in which parents perceived their main responsibility as passing on their standards of acceptable behaviour — religious, moral and social — to their children. The aim of the conscientious parent and educator was to instill virtue rather than produce happiness in their young charges.

There was also an emphasis on the formation of character and therefore on the usefulness of knowledge; a correlation between the education of the child and the conduct of the man. This didactic purpose was achieved through a series of instructive dialogues in which Mother distributed her offering of knowledge and social morality to her children in their isolated home in the Australian bush.

Furthermore, Charlotte Barton stressed the factual basis of *A Mother's Offering* as the work's 'principal merit'. [2] She seems to have regarded the writing of fiction as a dereliction of duty: 'You know mine are true narratives. I am not at liberty to invent'. [3]

The book's physical format matched this severity of tone. It was a modest, sober production, which did not contain anything as frivolous as illustrations. On the local publishing scene it remained an isolated curiosity for some years.

A similar severity and emphasis on fact was found in *The Australian Picture Pleasure Book* (1857). This was the first local book produced for Australian children that did

'The Southerly Buster coming through Sydney Heads' by Francis H. Grundy from The Demon McGuire, *Sydney, 1870.*
This was the first separately published piece of fantasy writing and illustration for young Australians.

contain illustrations. However, the enjoyment promised in its euphonious title was actually belied by its staid collection of wood-engravings culled from the newspaper press of the day. Indeed, without the brief introduction addressed to children, which is the only text the book contains, we would never realise that it was intended to please a young audience! The introduction particularly praised the 'extraordinary faith of the publishers' in believing 'that a sufficient number of copies of any Picture Book can be disposed of to cover the expenses of engraving, printing and publishing'. Although produced locally, the work was more an expression of pride in the burgeoning and civilised life of the colonies, designed to impress outsiders.

With both *A Mother's Offering* and *The Australian Picture Pleasure Book*, the tone of children's book publishing in nineteenth-century Australia seemed bleak and restricted. One of the earliest exceptions to this was Francis H. Grundy's *The Demon McGuire*, which was published in Sydney in 1870. The work was printed for the author/illustrator by a general firm of printers and contains 12 full-page lithographs on a fantasy theme.

This is the first major Australian piece of fantasy writing and illustrating for children and its imaginative impetus came from a uniquely local experience: the Southerly Buster sweeping through Sydney Heads becomes a mighty giant bestriding the Lilliputian colonists and wreaking havoc on their activities.

The most entertaining nineteenth-century work for Australian children, both textually

Cole's Patent Whipping Machine for Flogging Naughty Boys in School
from Cole's Funny Picture Book No. 1 (Melbourne, 1930s reprint). This bizarre image has cautioned and maybe even titillated generations of Australians.

One of E. W. Cole's publications from the 1890s: a welcome respite from the evangelical tone of much children's literature of the time.

and pictorially, was *Cole's Funny Picture Book*, published for Christmas 1879 by the Melbourne bookseller E. W. Cole. Although it was created in the same vein as *The Australian Picture Pleasure Book* — illustrations were taken from a wide variety of sources rather than being specially commissioned — it did at least deliver the delight promised in the title!

Cole's book has been called 'the only indigenous work (excluding *The Sentimental Bloke*) with which Australians of all classes and conditions are familiar'. [4] Much of the book's enduring appeal lies in the bizarre illustrations Cole concocted: the cat riding a bike; the eccentric human figures, which metamorphose into screws, animals and birds; the bewildering picture puzzles and a whole welter of factual information made more palatable by a generous sprinkling of fantastic illustrations. Cole's feast has continued to tempt young Australians for more than a century and perhaps no one image has entertained and cautioned and maybe even titillated us more than the 'Patent Whipping Machine for Flogging Naughty Boys in School'.

But the book's idiosyncratic scrapbook style of compilation did not encourage children's book illustration as an Australian occupation. Without a care of copyright, Cole helped himself to the illustrated press of the late nineteenth century, and with the addition of new captions compiled his 'Kindergarten Books', the first ongoing series of publications for Australian children.

E. W. Cole was a bookseller first and foremost rather than a publisher. In this

An extraordinary image from COLE'S FUNNY PICTURE BOOK.

Gum Leaves by Ethel Turner, Sydney, 1900.

respect he is kin to the Sydney pair of George Evans, who published *A Mother's Offering,* and J. R. Clarke, who published *The Australian Picture Pleasure Book.* Evans was a pioneering bookseller and stationer and Clarke was better known for music publishing and selling. The figure who emerges as the most significant nineteenth-century Australian bookseller cum publisher to consistently issue children's books was George Robertson of Melbourne. Unlike E. W. Cole he made a practice of promoting local writing and illustrating.

Robertson first started trading in 1852 and by 1855 had begun the publishing side of his business. The following year he issued an edition of James Bonwick's *Geography of Australia and New Zealand,* beginning a long interest in school textbooks and educational treatises. In 1871 Robertson published his first imaginative children's title, Cyrus Mason's *The Australian Christmas Story Book,* which was reissued the following year as *The Australian Story Book.*

Although George Robertson died in 1898, the company name continued for another two decades and between 1871 and 1921, George Robertson & Company published at least 16 imaginative children's books. The fact that this relatively small number spans a 50-year time period and still, by Australian standards, remains a noteworthy achievement, is indicative of the minor status of children's book publishing and its lack of economic viability at the time.

George Robertson & Company gave continued support to furthering and maintaining the early profile of Ida Rentoul as Australia's first major children's book illustrator. Between 1907 and 1913, they published six titles which she illustrated: *Gum Tree Brownie* by Tarella Quin (1907), *Australian Songs for Young and Old* by Annie R. Rentoul and Georgette Peterson (1907), *The Lady of the Blue Beads* by Annie R. Rentoul (1908), *Bush Songs of Australia* by Annie R. Rentoul and Georgette Peterson (1910), *Before the Lamps are Lit* by Tarella Quin (1911) and *More Australian Songs* by Annie R. Rentoul and Georgette Peterson (1913). Some of these titles were reprinted two or three times. This was the first major conjunction between an Australian publisher and illustrator and it established a precedent later followed by Angus &

'They pulled the fairies' beautiful hair' by George Lambert from THE SPIRIT OF THE BUSH FIRE, *Sydney, 1898. This was a much vaunted publication in its day, although Lambert's style was more suited to realism than fantasy.*

Robertson in Sydney with May Gibbs and Dorothy Wall.

In the 1890s competition between two Sydney firms contributed to the most professional production of Australian children's books in the nineteenth century. Angus & Robertson issued Louise Mack's *Teens* and *Girls Together* in 1897 and 1898 and Jessie Whitfeld's *The Spirit of the Bushfire* in 1898. William Brooks competed with *Bubbles, His Book* by R. F. Irvine in 1899 and *Gum Leaves* by Ethel Turner in 1900. Of these, the last three were fantasy titles and G. W. Lambert departed from his usual factual vision to contribute uncomfortably to Whitfeld's book. D. H. Souter, on the other hand, revelled in the opportunity to illustrate Brooks' titles and produced two little masterpieces.

The decade of the 1890s saw Australians themselves coming to the fore as authors and illustrators and these Sydney publications mark the first major attempt from local industry to compete with their English counterparts for a share of the local market. *The Spirit of the Bushfire* was proudly advertised by Angus & Robertson as a unique work: 'No such elaborate illustration has hitherto been attempted in Australia before.' [5]

The publisher's boast was directed at George Lambert's 32 black and white illustrations — his first and last excursion into the fantasy realm. His pedestrian illustrations featured fairies who resembled classically draped drawing-class models, solidly earth bound rather than ethereal and enchanting. Lambert's style actually sat

more comfortably with the commission from the publishers Angus & Robertson to illustrate Louise Mack's schoolgirl novel, *Girls Together.*

D. H. Souter's fantasy work, by contrast, was both decorative and whimsical and certain to enchant a young audience. The two titles he illustrated were also significant for their aesthetic design. Their format alone, embossed cloth on *Bubbles* and bold colour cover on *Gum Leaves,* shows how far removed they are from earlier nineteenth-century works less amenable to childish delight and interest. *Bubbles,* in fact, was as much a showcase of Australian printing excellence as it was of Souter's illustrations and was quite rightly praised as 'perhaps the most ambitious effort of an Australian [publishing] house by Australian men for Australian children'. [6]

Perhaps the only other locally produced children's book to adapt its format to a young audience was J. Takuma's *Kookaburra (The Laughing Jackass) and the Black Snake,* published in Sydney in 1897. This rare and little-known fantasy work tells of the deadly feud between these two denizens of the Australian bush and was presented in a booklet shaped to resemble an emu's egg!

Angus & Robertson began to establish their base of Australian children's classics in the 1890s and within 20 years the publishing centre for children's books had definitely moved from Melbourne to Sydney. After Angus & Robertson's sporadic start with *Teens* in 1894, other notable works followed: the first Australian editions of *Dot and the Kangaroo* in 1906 and 1913, the first anthologies of Australian poetry for children in 1913 and 1915, and six titles between 1913 and 1915 by Amy Eleanor Mack, the first local children's author to receive their constant encouragement.

The most significant of these six titles was *Scribbling Sue* (1913). Its colour frontispiece and four full-page black and white illustrations marked the arrival of a new artist on the Sydney scene, May Gibbs. This was May Gibbs' first major commission in Australia from a children's book publisher. The following year, she contributed a colour frontispiece to Constance Mackaness' *Gem of the Flat.* Angus & Robertson were now beginning to eclipse all other publishers in their production of Australian children's books.

There was, however, to be one last and magnificent challenge from the Melbourne scene, by the publishing firm of Lothians. In October 1916, amid a fanfare of publicity, they issued Ida Rentoul Outhwaite's long-awaited folio *Elves & Fairies.* Even today there is no more lavishly produced Australian children's book. Its 45 full-page

One of May Gibbs' earliest commissions on the Australian scene.

tipped-in illustrations established Outhwaite as Australia's most professional and sought-after illustrator. Once again local craftsmanship was seen as justifiable cause for comment:

We [the publishers] assured her [Ida] that there were in Victoria experts in the three and four colour process, who could make reproductions equivalent to anything in the old world, and, though it would mean an outlay unknown in the publishing history of Australia, we could bring out a book equal to anything ever placed before the public. [7]

Outhwaite's triumph was also to be maintained in one unique way: she inspired a Melbourne based 'Elves and Fairies' school of fantasy illustration and ranked among her followers Ethel Jackson Morris, Ethel Spowers, Christian Yandell and Edith Alsop. It was primarily this Melbourne fraternity working in an English idiom that gave Australian fantasy illustration an acknowledged place in the international genre. In the early 1900s the English fantasy school, and in particular the work of Arthur Rackham, Edmund Dulac and William Heath Robinson, was a recognised influence on these Melbourne illustrators and reviews of local work often drew on the names of such English counterparts for comparison and validation. The Melbourne fraternity even inspired Australia's equivalent to the Peter Pan statue in London's Kensington Gardens with Ola Cohn's Fairies Tree:

I have carved a tree in the Fitzroy Gardens for you and the fairies, but mostly for the fairies and those who believe in them, for they will understand how necessary it is to have a fairy sanctuary ...

Mainstream children's book publishing in Australia understandably dates from the publication of *Elves & Fairies*, although Angus & Robertson's offering for the year was almost the exact opposite of Lothian's 'tour de force'. May Gibbs' *Gumnut Babies* (1916) used only two colour plates in company with 11 monochrome plates and was presented as an item of mass appeal with a large print run rather than as a limited edition for subscribers.

May Gibbs' bushland mythology seemed to fulfill a timely imaginative need for Australian youth. Nature study for children

Opening illustration from May Gibbs' GUMNUT BABIES, Sydney, 1916. Like Beatrix Potter, May Gibbs showed an equal concern for balancing her text and illustrations in a format suitable for small hands.

'They came upon the flying foxes' by Elizabeth Durack from THE WAY OF THE WHIRLWIND, *Perth, 1941.*
The last of the grandly presented fantasy classics, it was published 100 years after Australia's first children's book appeared.

in Australia only became part of the formal school curricula at the beginning of the twentieth century. [8] The first 'readers', a series by William Gillies for Victorian schools (c.1902–1904), were widely adopted and used throughout Australia and while they contained an appropriate element of national pride they avoided undue sentiment. [9]

There is also evidence of an oral tradition in Australian children's folklore which, until 1916, had been denied a visual dimension:

The average bush youngster has a horror of darkness, and talks in awe-struck whispers of hairy men, ghosts and bunyips. This fear is inculcated from babyhood. The mother can't always be watching in a playground that is boundless, and she knows the horrors that wait the bushed youngster. So she tells them there is a bunyip in the lagoon, and gigantic eels in the creek; and beyond that hill there, and in yonder scrub, there is a 'bogey-man'. [10]

May Gibbs' creation of white Australia's first pictorial folklore for children seemed a spontaneous outcome from this evocative tradition and conquered the popular imagination with an almost mythic appeal.

If Melbourne's fantasy vision culminated in a 'fairy sanctuary', Sydney responded with typical idiosyncratic variety. From the Gumnut Babies, the Banksia Men, the Magic Pudding and Blinky Bill, Sydney's fantasy contribution is characterised by a boisterous, and perhaps more masculine vision. The 'Elves and Fairies' Melbourne vision exerted no charm for May Gibbs: she was quoted as saying that 'ordinary, conventional fairies with wands and starry crowns never did appeal to her'. [11] Her recourse to a powerful, almost subconscious national vocabulary did not inspire a school of bush fantasy. Her creation is a self-contained world, symbolised by the circle that surrounds her signature.

May Gibbs' combination of sheer originality, humour and an Australiana-based vision, which could be construed as patriotic, was an immediate contribution to Australia's pictorial propaganda and its wartime origins guaranteed national popularity. While Outhwaite's profile had taken a decade to establish, May Gibbs achieved success virtually overnight.

Linocut illustration by Marjorie Wood from THE FAIRIES' TREE Melbourne, 1932.

The sudden flourishing of illustrative talent and publishing initiative in Sydney pre-1920 was considerably activated by nationalistic fervour and wartime energy. Import restrictions threw national endeavour back on to its own resources and the printing trade, like others, became proudly Australian. An imaginative call to arms was answered by illustrators who could satisfy a demand for pictorial propaganda on all levels.

Perhaps the only other Australian fantasy vision that contained something of an indigenous vitality and rigour was that of Elizabeth Durack. Her *Way of the Whirlwind* (1941) was the last of the grandly presented fantasy classics and its lavish production was matched by an inspired vision that utilised Aboriginal motifs in a striking and sympathetic manner.

Durack's vision in her major illustrated book can be compared with that of Margaret Preston's, whose output in the 1940s was dominated by a search for the spiritual essence of Aboriginal art. This similar but independent reaction by two great Australian women artists has not been linked before and would repay more extended consideration.

The *Way of the Whirlwind* was reprinted three times before the end of the war and must certainly stand as the most strikingly produced and illustrated children's book issued in Australia in the 1940s. Its strong juxtaposition of colours, dramatic use of black and the sensuous curve of many of the compositions capture a unique vision of West Australia's Kimberley district. The book's arresting quality gave it a look more akin to the finely produced books of the 1920s than to the cheap wartime issues, which were common at this time.

These enduring classics of Australian fantasy illustration are considered in more detail in the following pages. Their part in shaping the culture of Australia's children and in giving them a wealth of evocative imagery is celebrated in a line of development from Ida Rentoul Outhwaite to the second generation as represented by Pixie O'Harris, Peg Maltby and Jean Elder.

Endnotes

1 Frederick B. Schell, How Books are Illustrated, *Centennial Magazine*, v.1 no.2, September 1888, p.121.

2 [Charlotte Barton], *A Mother's Offering to her Children*, (Sydney: 'Gazette Office', 1841), Preface.

3 Ibid, p.124.

4 Randolph Stow, 'Our Children in Cole Land', *Australian Letters*, v.1 no.3, April 1958, p.14.

5 *Bulletin*, 11 December 1897.

6 *Sydney Morning Herald*, 16 August 1899.

7 'Prospectus' for *Elves & Fairies*, Melbourne: Lothian, 1916.

8 Rosemary Polya, *Australian School Science Text-Books*, 1850–1939: *A Bibliography*, La Trobe University, Bundoora, Victoria: 1986, p.29.

9 Ibid, p.29.

10 Edward S. Sorenson, *Life in the Australian Backblocks*, London: Whitcombe & Tombs, 1911.

11 Quoted in Mary Marlowe, 'Mother of the gum nut babies: May Gibbs at home', *Women's World*, 1 December 1922, p.13.

'Scared of the Kewpies', a very early fantasy work by Ola Cohn, which shows the obvious influence of the nursery world of Mabel Lucie Attwell.

'Jilted' by D. H. Souter.

D. H. Souter

Australia's First Major Fantasy Illustrator

D. H. Souter was one of many whose talent and distinct contribution to black and white art in Australia has been overshadowed by Norman Lindsay. If Souter had displayed more of Norman Lindsay's personality, such as ambition and swaggering self-promotion, then his name might be better remembered today. If he had allowed his illustrative interest in the female form to override his consuming illustrative passion for the pattern, embellishment and design of their chic clothes and aesthetic domestic settings, then he might have maintained a profile as evocative as his fellow artist.

Souter, however, never deviated from his chosen path as an illustrator of modest books and cartoonist to the daily press. He preferred to work on a scale more suited to vignettes and on cartoons whose witty captions underscored the thrust and parry of social intercourse.

However, if the scale on which Souter worked was small his reputation in his day was considerable. It is time we looked at Souter's work afresh and saw him as one of the finest pen and ink artists in Australia's history.

David Henry Souter (1862–1935) was born in Aberdeen, Scotland, and seems to have been a self-taught artist and journalist. This dual ability with the pen was one of Souter's most striking characteristics. He served an apprenticeship as a house painter and decorator, studied briefly at a branch of the South Kensington School in Aberdeen and joined the staff of the *Bon Accord*, reputedly the first illustrated paper in Scotland. While still a teenager he travelled to South Africa with his family and after five unprofitable years left for Australia. In February 1885, just prior to his departure, he married Janet Swanson and they arrived in Melbourne later that year. In 1887 they moved permanently to Sydney where D. H. Souter

EVERY MAN IN HIS HUMOUR.
'Don't go in there, dear! Dada's cross.'
'What's the matter with him?'
'He's drawing funny pictures to make people laugh.'
BULLETIN cartoon, 1 MARCH 1902.

quickly assimilated into its cultural and social life.

At the time, technical limitations in reproductive processes were being overcome by innovative photographic methods. These enabled every nuance of pen and ink work to be copied, without resorting to the interpretative burden of engraving. D. H. Souter was one of the first to exploit the new methods and introduce the fluidity and sophistication of the Art Nouveau line into a cartooning field formerly dominated by less flamboyant and heavier woodcut-derived styles.

Illustration from B. P. MAGAZINE, 1 March 1934.

Souter was a young man with energy and social skills and he found a ready outlet in the vital art community of late Victorian Sydney. In April 1888 he founded the Brush Club associated with the Art Society of New South Wales and in August 1895 he was elected to the first Council of the Society of Artists. He served as its President from 1901 to 1902. Between 1904 and 1911 he acted as art editor for *Art & Architecture* and as such was one of the pioneers of art journalism in Australia.

D. H. Souter was a prominent local identity, yet he never achieved the nation-wide stature of Norman Lindsay, May Gibbs or Ida Rentoul Outhwaite. Unfortunately his illustrative work was not enshrined in classic texts which would have kept his name to the fore over generations of young readers. He was never seduced into appearing in the pages of deluxe editions

Captivating Caricatures of Cats

[IN ROYAL DOULTON WARE].

Doulton Ware Vase, Jugs, Tobacco Jar and Candlestick.

Vases, Ewer shape, 8½ ins., cream colour 5/9

Vases, assorted shapes, 6in., cream colour 5/6, 8 in. 6/9, 9½in 6/9

Jugs, assorted shapes, cream colour... ... ... 2/9 and 3/-

Tobacco Jars, assorted shapes, cream colour 6/6

Teapots (large size), cream colour 4/6

Teapots (medium size), cream colour 3/9

Teapots (small size), cream colour 3/3

Children's Mugs, yellow, green or lemon shade, large 2/3, small 2/-

Baby's Plate, cream colour only 2/6

Porridge Bowls, yellow, green or lemon shade 3/3

Plaques, cream colour, a series of six, illustrating various phases of cat life each .. 2/3

Breakfast Cups and Saucers, yellow, green or lemon shade .. .. each .. 4/9

Tea Cups and Saucers, yellow, green or lemon shade each 3/6

Coffee Cups and Saucers, yellow, green or lemon shade .. .. each .. 3/-

Tea Plates, yellow, green or lemon shade .. ..each .. 3/-

Tea Plates (Afternoon), yellow, green or lemon shade each .. 2/-

Tall Candlesticks, Scotch style, 9in. high, cream colour 6/6

Cats, 13in. high, green and yellow colour, exquisitely modelled 15/6

Full Illustrated Price List Post Free on Request.

FARMER'S FARMER & COMPANY LIMITED SYDNEY.

Advertisement in SOCIETY OF ARTISTS SPRING EXHIBITION CATALOGUE, August 1907.

for collectors of fine printings, and he never outraged authority by salacious and large satiric pen drawings. Without the stimulus of major commissions, he turned out a welter of consistently stylish work for textbooks, short-lived magazines, cartoons and ephemera. His contributions to the *Bulletin* alone could number several thousand.

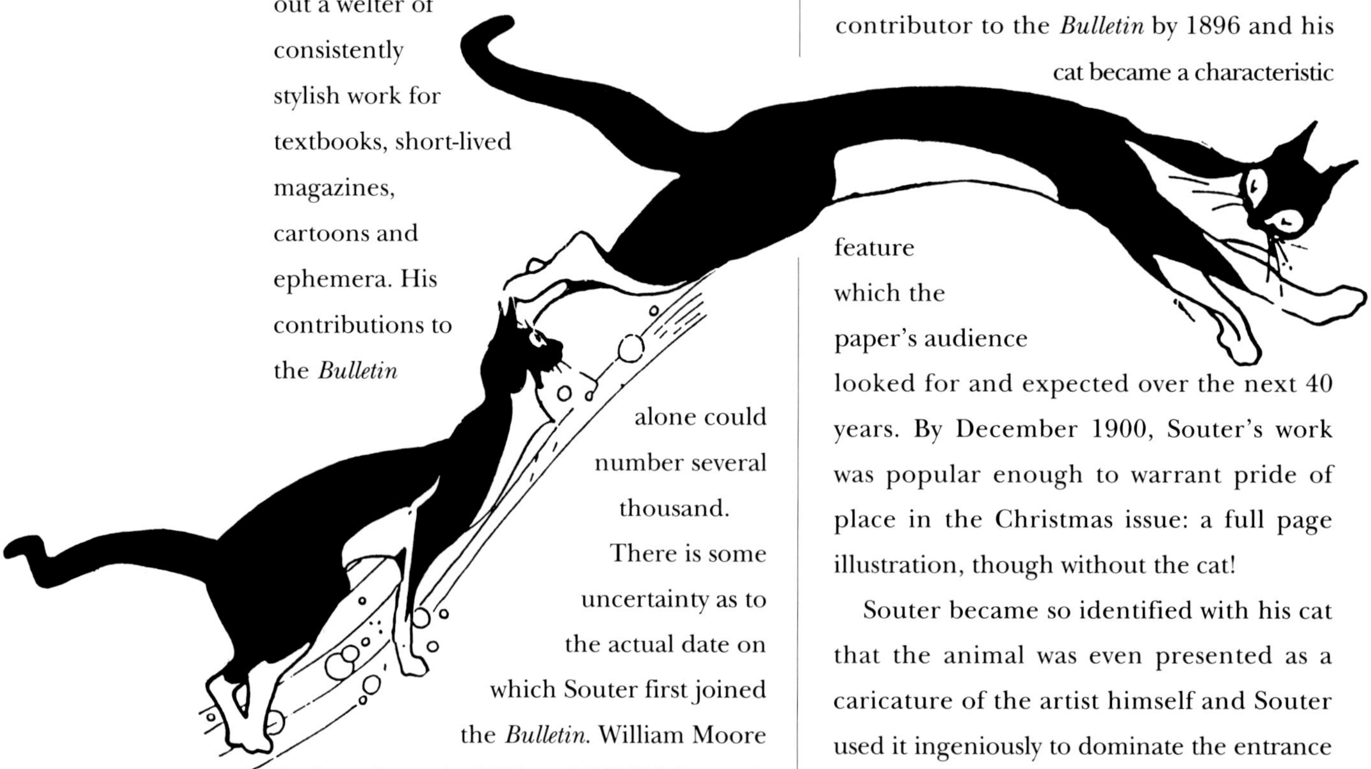

There is some uncertainty as to the actual date on which Souter first joined the *Bulletin*. William Moore declares it was in 1892 and 1896! [1] Souter's first contribution to the *Bulletin* actually appeared on 23 February 1895. Less than 6 months later, on 27 July a cartoon of his appeared featuring a cat — it was to become his trademark. It has been said that Souter's cat was the product of an accident:

One day a large blob of ink landed on a drawing which he had just finished. He was too tired to start another, so with the aid of some Chinese white, he transformed the black mass into a cat. [2]

Souter's own explanation was much more prosaic:

... it happened that a sketch I was doing for the Bulletin *needed a blob of black to balance the composition, so I put in the cat, and when the drawing appeared several people talked. Some thought it clever ...* [3]

Whatever the truth of either story, D. H. Souter was established as a regular contributor to the *Bulletin* by 1896 and his cat became a characteristic feature which the paper's audience looked for and expected over the next 40 years. By December 1900, Souter's work was popular enough to warrant pride of place in the Christmas issue: a full page illustration, though without the cat!

Souter became so identified with his cat that the animal was even presented as a caricature of the artist himself and Souter used it ingeniously to dominate the entrance to his studio:

You reached his King Street studio by four flights of stairs, round the walls of which wound the enormously elongated body of that cat, beginning with its bushy tail at the street entrance and ending with a viciously smiling head that poked out its tongue in the direction of the studio door. [4]

The only other black and white artist in Australia who consistently worked within the Art Nouveau mode and whose illustrations also appeared in the *Bulletin* was Ian Gall (1904–1981). Gall's work derived from Aubrey Beardsley and other Art Nouveau revival illustrators and his decadence seems forced and out of place in an Australian context. Ultimately it highlights

Souter's own imaginative skills and compositional strengths. On the international scene, the extremely popular English illustrator and cartoonist Louis Wain (1890–1939) built his reputation entirely upon the depiction of feline antics. Wain's cats first appeared in the mid 1880s and by the following decade were eagerly sought out in the pages of the *Illustrated London News.* Both Souter and Wain were using their cats to satirical and witty effect. However, Wain's humanised figures of elegant cats in evening dress, sporting monocles and cigars are far removed from Souter's sophisticated creations, which never lose their essential feline nature. Wain's work remains of interest only as a document in the history of kitsch.

The Souter cat did not limit its appearance solely to the pages of the *Bulletin.* It appeared in numerous magazines, on postcards, book-plates, in book illustrations and in advertisements. In 1906 it first appeared on a range of Doulton ware — a remarkable distinction which attests to the creature's international appeal:

All sorts and conditions of cats gambol and sleep and prowl in graceful attitudes for the purpose of decorating a teacup or a vase, and strangely-contorted cats, of a delicate grey, entwine themselves with sinuous grace in a border that has all the rhythmic movement of an antique frieze ... [5]

In June that year, one of Souter's cartoons in the *Bulletin* included a large vase decorated with a sinuous spiral of cats. This stylish ornament could very easily have come from the pages of the Doulton catalogue itself!

'IT IS THE CAUSE, IT IS THE CAUSE, MY SOUL!'
'Adelina Footytes, what makes you so hard?' 'Years of dealing with theatrical managers, dear boy.'
BULLETIN cartoon
3 DECEMBER 1898.

The cat also appeared in the children's magazine *Young Australia* and in its day became as recognisable an Australian icon as May Gibbs' gumnut babies and Jimmie Bancks' Ginger Meggs. Coincidentally, another famous cartoon cat, Felix, also sprang from the fertile mind of an Australian — Pat Sullivan (1887–1933).

Souter's famous cat, sometimes to be seen toying with a mouse, had an obvious affinity with the young women of Souter's cartoons who toyed with the affections and sensibilities of the Australian male or deftly

AFTER THE 'RAZZLE'
'Brace up, old man, I'll have to be off or my wife won't speak to me when I get home.'
'Lucky dog. Mine — hic! — 'll talk to me all night.
BULLETIN cartoon
29 August 1896.

batted 'catty' rejoinders back with the flick of an obvious, albeit well-gloved, claw. As one of Souter's own poems succinctly said:

Man's merely an animal
(No doubt of that)
Who likes being purred to, and:-
Woman's the CAT. [6]

The cat serves as a female sexual metonym, as well as acting the role of a cynical chorus to each confrontation, in which it immediately catches the viewer's eye. The cat always suits the atmosphere of each cartoon: its impeccable black and white visage is as sartorially correct as any of the gentlemen in their starched white shirt fronts and black coats. The sinuous line of the cat and its snaking tail become part of a larger composition in which curves and arabesques echo the interweaving of other social animals. Souter's women, from kitchen-maid to 'femme fatale', are distinct and original pictorial types and in the illustrative tradition which vaunts such

COMPETITION
Barke: 'My wife and I never quarrel. What you thinka that?'
Clarke: 'Not bad! Now I'll tell one.'
BULLETIN cartoon 21 APRIL 1927.

THE
LONE HAND
THE AUSTRALIAN
MONTHLY
Price 1/-
SEPT. 1909

comparative (American) examples as 'The Gibson Girl' and 'The Harrison Fisher Girl', it is surely time that 'The Souter Girl' received her due recognition!

creators of this pictorial imbalance. Such urban themes as were depicted by Phil May (1864–1903) and later by Alf

A MOONLIGHT EPISODE
TOM: 'Say, Maria, these folks must think we've been getting married!'
BULLETIN cartoon
19 SEPTEMBER 1896.

Although by the turn of the twentieth century more than two-thirds of the Australian population lived an urban life, the cartoons in the *Bulletin* were still dominated by outback types and bush life. Frank Mahony (1862–1917) and George Lambert (1873–1930) were the principal

THE CHARM OF VARIETY
'Don't you know any other step besides this one?'
'Sure I do—kick with the other foot.'
BULLETIN cartoon
5 MAY 1927.

Vincent (1874–1915), tended to concentrate on the low-life of the city. D. H. Souter could therefore justifiably claim to be the first *Bulletin* artist who consistently depicted an urban life that concentrated on the middle-class or those with middle-class pretentions, the newspaper's urban audience. If politics interested Souter it was the politics of the household and its internecine struggles; if rural types appeared in his work they were more likely to be engaged in the battle of the sexes rather than fighting a hostile outback. While other *Bulletin* cartoonists caught the popular imagination by contributing to a national legend of nineteenth-century origin, D. H. Souter helped Australians formulate not just a twentieth-century image of themselves, but also one that revealed their developing cosmopolitan bonds. The social similarities of Sydney's city dwellers to their counterparts elsewhere,

THE KANGAROO CAT, or the Katgaroo,
Has, so far, only been seen by few.
For Somebody, only the other day, drew
The identical one that is looking at you.

'There's no such animal,' Somepeople said:
Somebody smiled and nodded his head.

'You have Kangaroo Rat,
So why shouldn't you
Have Kangaroo Cats
Or a Katgaroo?'

Bush-Babs, Sydney, 1933.

the same pretentions and foibles, were all grist to Souter's mill and guaranteed a widespread appeal.

Souter's *Bulletin* cartoons provide the most accessible chronicle of the long-term career of any professional Australian illustrator and cartoonist. Unlike other late nineteenth-century Australian newspaper illustrators, Souter was not merely following a vocation by default or force of economic circumstance. Nor was his profession a subsidiary pursuit, prelude or training ground to a later exhibiting career in 'high art'. Souter remained committed to his metier and his 40 years of contributions to the *Bulletin* confirm this commitment . Style and humour are always present in his work, which never became stale or predictable. It constantly developed, moving from Art Nouveau to Art Deco, and always retained its integrity. The fact that its humour has remained vital is as much a tribute to Souter's graphic flair as it is to his wit and mastery of the succinct caption.

Vignette illustration by D.H. Souter from BUBBLES*, Sydney, 1899.*

After an initial and understandable flirtation with an Aubrey Beardsley influence, Souter settled into an individual style noted for its use of solid black and white areas, relieved by fine ornamentation. Although he was always fascinated by the decorative excesses of women's clothes, his models are usually juxtaposed against the starkly unadorned clothes and solid presence of males. Souter never stinted on any of his illustrative work, but there is always an economy of line and an overriding rhythm to the design of each illustration. Equally characteristic is his willingness to experiment with unusual shapes for his illustrations, to position them to dramatic and decorative effect within the text itself and to use a viewing angle that is arresting and original.

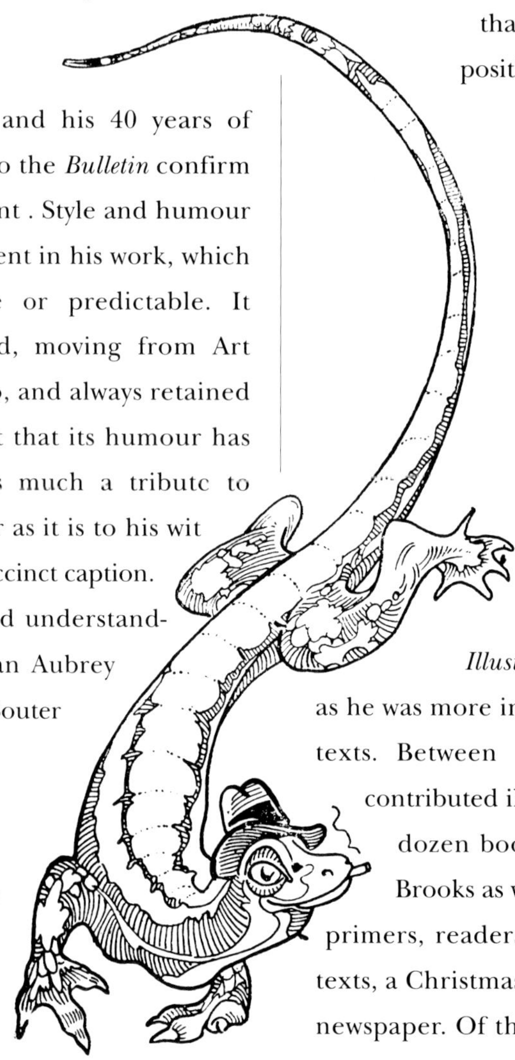

Souter worked for John Sands for more than a decade before taking a position with William Brooks as manager of their art department. His indefatigable energy was expended on vignette illustrations, illuminated addresses and calligraphic work, book covers, advertising art, illustrations for children's and adult's books and textbooks. He was as ready to illustrate *Muskett's Illustrated Medical Guide* (1903) as he was more imaginative and exuberant texts. Between 1898 and 1922, Souter contributed illustrations to more than a dozen books published by William Brooks as well as to a series of school primers, readers, geography and history texts, a Christmas Annual and a children's newspaper. Of these, the most lavish were

'The Chariot of the Great Magician' by D. H. Souter from BUBBLES, *Sydney, 1899.*

ENDEAVOUR
PRESS

AUSTRALIAN
Bush-Babs
with Pictures
by
D·H·SOUTER
2/-

both children's books: Robert Irvine's *Bubbles, His Book* (1899) and Ethel Turner's *Gum Leaves* (1900).

Bubbles is remembered today only for its illustration and design, which make it a milestone in Australian children's book production. A short version of the story with only black and white illustrations was initially serialised in five issues of *The Children's Newspaper* (1899). The adventurous decision to issue an expanded version in lavish format with full-page colour plates gave Souter an ideal opportunity to showcase his illustrative talent as well as exercise his book design skills. *Bubbles* was reissued in a London edition one year after its publication in Australia — the first time an Australian children's illustrated book was so validated by an appreciative English audience.

Illustration by D. H. Souter from BUSH-BABS.

Why did it appeal to an international audience? It was certainly not due to any idiosyncratic Australian touch. *Bubbles* probably assimilated well into the English scene by satisfying the current vogue for children's books that drew on the aesthetic design principles of Walter Crane and the decorative appeal of the Art Nouveau movement.

Crane's theories of book design had been popularised in the 1896 work, *Of the Decorative Illustration of Books Old and New.* He presented the ideal book as an integrated whole. The relationship of binding, cover design, endpapers and other preliminaries to one another and to the rest of the book was considered as important as arranging illustrations to suit the format and choosing an appropriate typeface. Souter eagerly adopted these principles and *Bubbles* is very much a showcase of Australian printing excellence and design skills. There is an inventiveness, even a playfulness, evident in the typographical layout, in the cover design and in the vignette illustrations. Unfortunately, the addition by the printer of flat areas of colour to the full-page illustrations makes Souter's original conceptions in black and white appear overworked. Like Ida Rentoul Outhwaite a generation later, Souter did not need colour to enhance his work.

Perhaps the most effective colour illustration is 'The Chariot of the Great Magician', in which a dizzying aerial perspective is conveyed by the large unbroken areas of the eagles' wings, which overlie the minute shifting detail beneath. But it is the numerous, smaller black and white illustrations that attract most attention today now that colour printing has reached such sophisticated standards.

Casting aside this retrospective evaluation, *Bubbles* would have emerged as a daring and fascinating achievement to an 1890s audience. Colour printing did not become an expected part of Australian children's books until at least after 1916, when Lothians issued Outhwaite's *Elves & Fairies*. In its day *Bubbles* was praised as 'perhaps the most ambitious effort of an Australian [publishing] house by Australian men for Australian children.' [7]

The next year, *Bubbles* was followed by *Gum Leaves*, which was illustrated entirely in black and white. Souter's own expertise in verbal ingenuity and wordplay was more than matched by Ethel Turner. He was inspired by her short tales, verses and journalistic snippets, which were far more engrossing than Robert Irvine's text for *Bubbles*.

After these publications, however, Souter did not go on to maintain a profile as a children's book illustrator or book designer. His work was constantly in demand, but it was his weekly contributions to the *Bulletin* that consolidated his position as a leading black and white artist and humorist. During the First World War, his contribution to pictorial propaganda was every bit as trenchant as Norman Lindsay's and two collections of his work were gathered for publication. This unjustly forgotten aspect of Souter's work deserves separate consideration for its savage satire and biting effect.

Throughout the 1920s, significant changes occurred in his subject matter and style. He broadened his themes to reflect a direct change in Sydney's social life — domestic scenes still predominated in his cartoons, but there was also a developing interest in scenes set at the beach. Souter had introduced this theme as early as 1905 but by the 1920s, the outdoor occupations of his

Illustration from BUSH-BABS.

contemporaries were being consistently surveyed by his amused eye.

Souter's stylistic change was characterised by a move from the flowing line of Art Nouveau to the more angular and simplified Art Deco. This change was gradual and harmonious and for the last decade of Souter's output, there are a large number of drawings in this mode. One can only wonder why his talents were not utilised to grace the covers of *The Home* magazine at this time for he would surely have produced designs as striking as those offered by Adrian Feint, Hera Roberts and Thea Proctor, all of whom incorporated the Art Deco mode.

More than 20 years after *The Children's Newspaper* gave Souter his first opportunity to revel in illustration for a young audience, another magazine similarly utilised his talents. Between 1928 and 1929 the Sydney magazine *Young Australia* produced a series of full-page nursery rhymes written and illustrated by Souter. He presented them in a distinctive calligraphic script and set them around an eye-catching illustration. The impetus for this project had been the *Bulletin's* competition in 1917 to encourage Australian nursery rhymes. From more than 1000 entries, two of Souter's rhymes had been chosen for inclusion in a modest booklet: *Australian Nursery Rimes.*

Almost all of this nursery rhyme series was included, some rewritten and re-illustrated, in Souter's last book, *Bush-Babs* (1933). The depressed 1930s in Australia were not a productive time for children's books: Outhwaite's vision had been over-worked, and May Gibbs was restricted to reissues of earlier works and her weekly comic strips. The most significant new-comer in this period was Dorothy Wall with her uniformly produced Blinky Bill series.

Vignette illustration by D. H. Souter from GUM LEAVES, *Sydney, 1900.*

Souter's *Bush-Babs* injected a breath of fresh air into this field. The book's strength lay in more than 40 years of professional training and the economic use of language and line, both invested with humour appreciated by adult and child alike. *Bush-Babs* looked nothing like the familiar children's picture books Australia had been producing for more than a decade. Its elongated format was presumably designed to suit the illustrations rather than the reverse, its lack of colour illustrations was offset by a remarkable wrap-around colour cover of striking design and its textual illustrations were intertwined throughout the text, which was itself laid out in imaginative blocks.

Bush-Babs was Souter's swan song and its wit and style makes it as arresting and amusing today as it was 50 years ago.

ENDNOTES

1 William Moore, *The Story of Australian Art,* v.1, Sydney, 1934, p.240; William Moore, 'D. H. S.,"A Prodigious Worker"', *Sydney Morning Herald,* 5 October 1935, p.13.

2 William Moore, op. cit., v. 2, p.116.

3 'The Bulletin Zoo', *Bulletin,* 10 December 1908, Red Page.

4 Arthur W. Jose, *The Romantic Nineties,* Sydney, 1933, p.25.

5 N.E.W., 'New Doulton Ware: Australian Art and English Craftsmen', *Art & Architecture,* v.3 no.4, 1906, p.157.

6 D. H. Souter, *Bulletin,* 2 October 1897, p.11.

7 *Sydney Morning Herald,* 16 August 1899.

Verse and illustration by D. H. Souter from AUSTRALIAN NURSERY RIMES*, 1917.*

'The Secret Pool' by Ida Rentoul Outhwaite.

Ida Rentoul Outhwaite

International Fantasy Illustrator

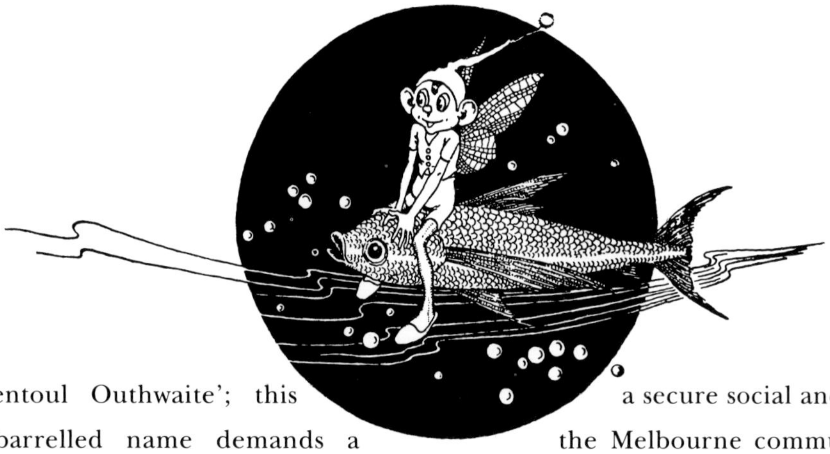

'Ida Rentoul Outhwaite'; this triple-barrelled name demands a considered enunciation. It has a lilt and romanticism that accords well with the fact she was named after the figure in Tennyson's poem 'The Princess'. It has, by contrast, none of the more abrupt and business-like sound of 'May Gibbs'.

To many of her admirers, Ida Outhwaite's life and career, or at least the popular conception of them, read like a fairytale. It was as if her illustrative talent had been bestowed at birth: 'the gift was born with her'. [1] Her first published drawings appeared in 1903 when she was only fifteen. Publishers clamoured for her work, English Royalty purchased her drawings and her real world seemed to appropriate much of the perfection of her fantasy world.

In the popular imagination, Ida remains a dilettantish figure, part of a sheltered family environment with a secure social and intellectual standing in the Melbourne community. Her extraordinary solo exhibition profile (extraordinary not just for a children's book illustrator but for an untrained Australian woman artist), her celebrity status and her 'de luxe' presentation in print all combined to establish an image far removed from that of the hard-working illustrator.

The truth, of course, is far less romantic. There is often a tendency to equate any creative personality with their work. In the case of a children's book illustrator this trivialising process can meet its most absurd reduction. Ida did much more than wave a wand for her books and illustrations to be produced from what one belittling critic called the 'Fairy Factory'.

Ida Rentoul Outhwaite (1888–1960), born Ida Sherbourne Rentoul, developed her forte of pen and ink work at the same time that a discernible school of black and white art was established in Australia. In its formative stages, 1907–1911, her work appeared briefly in magazines in company with illustrations by Alex Sass, Percy and Ruby Lindsay and Ambrose Dyson senior. More than once Ruby Lindsay and Ida Outhwaite were favourably linked as promising young artists of the day. Outhwaite, however, was never really part of this or any other artistic group and perhaps her greatest affinity with the Lindsays was her consuming passion for self expression:

Vignette illustration by Ida Rentoul Outhwaite from ELVES & FAIRIES, *Melbourne, 1916.*

... before she was two years old, she drew birds ... and Noah's Ark men, women and beasts. She copied, with pencil and slate, the pictures on her nursery walls ... She and her older sister, Annie R. Rentoul, spent most of their time in early childhood drawing, painting, scribbling verses, grave and gay, collaborating with their brothers in little magazines, blood-thirsty adventure stories and bushranger-plays. [2]

'The witches ride on their brooms tonight' by Ida Rentoul Outhwaite from ELVES & FAIRIES.

Outhwaite received definitive guidance and inspiration for this passion by studying the same leading English illustrators in black and white who established standards for the Lindsays:

It was when I was eleven that someone gave me a bottle of Indian ink and some Gillot nibs and I discovered the bliss of working in black and white, which always has been and always will be my favourite medium ... Friends were very good in giving me the works of masters in black and white. I developed a passion, which I still keep for Phil May, and poured over Beardsley and Daniel Vierge. I also greatly admired Gordon Browne, and used to try his crosshatching, but have never been successful with it. [3]

Apart from Beardsley's example, however, these realist artists only supplied her with a technique of line control and with developing the nuances of texture and tone; they could not turn her vision from fantasy work.

Outhwaite had neither an Australian tradition of children's book illustration on which to base her vision, nor a collection of classic Australian texts to interpret for a new generation. The classic English children's texts that were available were seen to have been definitively illustrated by such figures as Arthur Rackham, Edmund Dulac, and Kay Nielsen. Her predicament was a considerable burden for an ambitious Australian illustrator. She solved this problem by getting family members to provide texts to her illustrations. However, the creative direction of her publications was therefore in reverse to the more usual situation where illustrations are inspired by an existing text.

'Keep her in our cavern for our queen!' by Ida Rentoul Outhwaite from THE LITTLE GREEN ROAD TO FAIRYLAND*, 1922.*

'Round the nursery they circled ... Fairies, and Elves, and Sprites, and Pixies' by Ida Rentoul from
The Lady of the Blue Beads. 1908.

'Trailing his nets from the crescent boat' by Ida Rentoul Outhwaite from BEFORE THE LAMPS ARE LIT *Melbourne, 1911.*

Even so, more than a decade before May Gibbs' first gumnut booklet appeared in 1916, the illustrations of Ida Rentoul steadily popularised her name and her fairyland vision across Australia. She became the first locally-born illustrator to produce a significant body of children's books. Outhwaite's pictorial style, which was largely derived from English example, established a nationally recognised fantasy vision in Australia which stood virtually unchallenged for more than a decade. Her folio-sized masterpiece — aptly entitled *Elves & Fairies* — appeared in 1916, and by an extraordinary coincidence, May Gibbs' diminutive series of five gumnut booklets also began publication that same year. Thereafter, two quite dissimilar fantasy visions dominated Australian children's books until the Depression.

Between 1904 and 1911, Ida Rentoul Outhwaite produced eight major books with black and white illustrations and developed an assured and individual technique as well as a repertoire of compositional devices. All these attributes are seen in the most successful work of this period: *Before the Lamps are Lit,* by Tarella Quin (Melbourne, George Robertson, 1911).

One particular illustration from this book, 'Trailing his nets from the crescent boat', warrants close attention. This work features one of Outhwaite's most favoured and most successful pictorial devices — the crescent boat. In this illustration its imaginative refinement results in what is

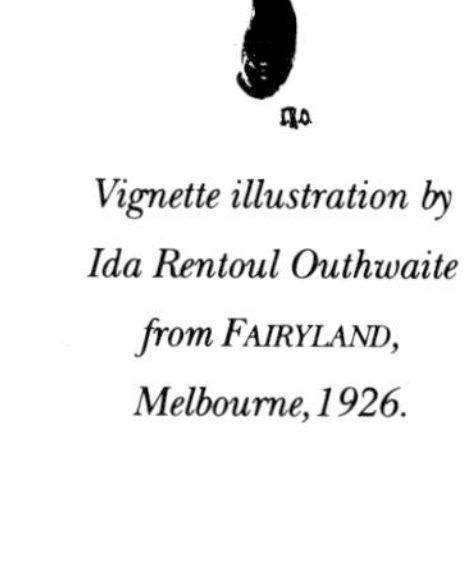

Vignette illustration by Ida Rentoul Outhwaite from FAIRYLAND, *Melbourne, 1926.*

'Periwinkle painting the petals' by Ida Rentoul Outhwaite from THE LITTLE FAIRY SISTER*, London, 1923.*

'Autumn Fairy' by Ida Rentoul Outhwaite from ELVES & FAIRIES.

undoubtedly her first technical 'tour de force'. Against a deep black sky the stark simplicity of the boat and its sails is contrasted with a variety of ornamentation and filigree detail. Outhwaite's exuberant technical assurance is shown to good effect in a variety of means used to depict texture: the old man's wispy beard, the different cross-hatchings of the net and the pin-prick bubbles.

Perhaps the only other illustrators of children's books with comparable black and white expertise at the time were the English brothers Charles and Heath Robinson. In an Australian context, Outhwaite's skills were second to none. Even D. H. Souter, another black and white master, was using a broader line to achieve less ornamented, if not equally effective work.

If her developing talent was centred in the creation of a black and white art tradition in Australia, it was also even more significantly part of the development of Australian children's book publishing.

Before the Lamps are Lit was her fifth major work to be published by George Robertson and highlights the fact that Australian children's book publishing was clearly centred in Melbourne at the time. It was not until 1916 that this geographical emphasis was firmly, and finally, re-established in Sydney with Angus & Robertson's publication of May Gibbs' titles. With the publication of *Elves & Fairies* in 1916, it looked as if this high point of children's book production could hardly be surpassed. But Angus & Robertson completely confounded such expectations by catering to the opposite end of the market and producing a series of ephemeral gumnut booklets of mass appeal.

For the moment, however, Australian children's books were almost entirely the trivial by-product of printing houses, or isolated examples such as Angus & Robertson's first children's book *Teens* in 1896. The one exception (if we exclude E. W. Cole's children's books) was Melbourne's George Robertson. His first imaginative children's book [4] was *The Australian Christmas Story Book* of 1871. Thereafter, and until 1921 when he amalgamated with Melville & Mullens, this firm issued a steady and select number of children's books, school textbooks and educational treatises. Their pioneering achievement in this direction has never been given the historical recognition it deserves and their promotion of Ida's work was integral to her success and popularity.

Ida Rentoul Outhwaite's position at the forefront of black and white art and children's book publishing in Australia was confirmed in October 1916 when *Elves & Fairies* was issued. With this volume we finally entered her fully realised fantasy vision. Seventy-five years later it is still the most impressive and sought after of all Australian children's illustrated books. The folio-sized volume was limited to 1500 copies, signed by Outhwaite, with a list of subscribers headed by the Governor-General of Australia. It contained 15 full-page colour plates, 30 full-page black and white plates (all tipped in) and numerous vignette illustrations, and was enclosed between decorated endpapers and bound within cloth boards embellished with a

'Oh, come away,' said Winkle, 'they'll never agree' by Ida Rentoul Outhwaite from CHIMNEY TOWN*, 1934.*

'Mr Merman and his Daughter' by Ida Rentoul Outhwaite from THE LITTLE FAIRY SISTER.

gold-blocked design. The only comparable production, *The Art of Frederick McCubbin* was also published by Lothians six months earlier. With hindsight, it is possible to see that both these works set standards for the steady growth of the Australian art press. [5]

Elves & Fairies far surpassed George Robertson's pioneering efforts and demands consideration as an art book first and foremost; an audience of children was virtually a minor consideration! This elevation of Outhwaite's work was appreciated in the most perceptive review of the book, which appeared in the *Bulletin.* It realised that Annie Rentoul's verses were written 'merely to illustrate her sister's pictures' and that they had a 'subordinate function.' [6] The *Bulletin* stated quite categorically, '*Elves & Fairies* claims attention as an art publication [and] ... undoubtedly ... deserves to be ranked with the important artistic productions in Australia'.

Outhwaite seemed capable of meeting every challenge her evolving career demanded. She added an accomplished use of water-colour to her repertoire, although her best black and white work hardly needed this extra embellishment, so bedazzling was its ornamentation and contrasting textures. Her favoured setting for showing this extraordinary facility with the pen was a night-time scene with a full moon riding in a striated sky; down below her fantasy figures capered against a dense black landscape. Silhouettes, particularly those of clutching ti-trees rendered with a thick and broken calligraphic line, provided a telling contrast to the delicate tracery of fairy figures.

Ida Rentoul Outhwaite's work had now been before the public since 1903 and its elevation to fine art status was most assuredly stage-managed by her husband's business acumen. Grenbry Outhwaite's enthusiasm moved her on to a new plateau as a major exhibiting artist and between 1916 and 1933, she held at least 18 one-woman exhibitions, usually coupled with launchings of her books. Unlike May Gibbs and Dorothy Wall, Ida Rentoul Outhwaite had a career that could be compared to international figures on the children's book scene. She achieved much more than local fame and popularity. One can only wonder just what May Gibbs might have achieved if, as she had hoped, her husband had also been an astute business manager.

Vignette illustration by Ida Rentoul Outhwaite from THE ENCHANTED FOREST, *London, 1921.*

Outhwaite's breakthrough on to the international scene came in 1920 when she achieved an ambition that had been thwarted by the war. An exhibition at the Fine Art Society Galleries in London in May introduced her work to an appreciative audience, including Queen Mary. With this strategic showing, she went on to conquer the publishing scene in London. A. & C. Black were to become her English promoters just as George Robertson had been a decade earlier in Australia. Eventually, A. & C. Black were to issue ten of her books — six new titles and four that

Vignette illustration by Ida Rentoul Outhwaite from BLOSSOM, *London, 1928.*

'She saw a little witch dance past' by Ida Rentoul from THE LADY OF THE BLUE BEADS, *1908.*

'Flower Frocks' by Ida Rentoul Outhwaite.

reprinted some of her earlier illustrations with different texts — and maintain their association with her until 1947. Throughout the 1920s they also popularised her work via a series of 48 colour postcards. In this way her imagery reached an incredibly wide audience. Ultimately, Ida Rentoul Outhwaite's illustrative contribution to the post-war decade in English publishing was the most significant of any new arrival.

Outhwaite's ready acceptance into the highly competitive fairy book market of the 1920s was not only due to her technical and imaginative excellence. Her work assimilated perfectly into English nurseries that had, ever since *Peter Pan*, maintained the cult of the fairy figure as playtime companion to the young. In the cossetted Edwardian nursery world, it was almost a duty to believe in fairies.

Peter Pan, which was first staged at Christmas 1904, offered more than a rhetorical question when it asked: 'Do you believe in fairies? ... If you believe, clap your hands!' It is reported that the audience at this opening night, significantly composed almost entirely of adults, responded spontaneously. *Peter Pan* the play, and later still the book version (1911), energised the Edwardian fashion for fairy literature, illustration and nursery decoration.

These fairies were not the spirited and grotesque hobgoblins or majestic demigods of the late nineteenth century, but a new species entirely. 'They had been waiting at the bottom of the garden with the appearance of little seven-year-old girls dressed, as no self-respecting mother would ever let their own daughters be dressed, in the flimsiest tulles of an almost immodest shortness.'[7] What is significant is that this new species was almost entirely childlike itself and so offered a ready source of identification with their young audience.

By the 1920s in England this fashion was reaching its full-blown heights: the Cottingley 'fairy' photographs, the flower fairy characters popularised by Margaret Tarrant and Cicely Mary Barker, the fairy poetry of Rose Fyleman and the whimsical illustrations of Mabel Lucie Attwell were all immensely popular phenomena of the 1920s.

The willing suspension of disbelief which made no less a person than Sir Arthur Conan Doyle the champion for the Cottingley 'fairy' photographs was eagerly embraced. Even the Australian press devoted considerable space to serious discussion on the subject.[8] Flower fairies in text and in pictures bloomed prolifically throughout the 1920s and Ida Rentoul Outhwaite later unashamedly emulated the English talent of Margaret Tarrant and Cicely Mary Barker in her own *Bunch of Wildflowers* (1933). Rose Fyleman's 'There are fairies at the bottom of our garden!' was originally written for the adult audience of *Punch* in 1917, and created a vogue for fairy poetry throughout the next decade. Mabel Lucie Attwell and a 1920s host of illustrators (usually women) continued to depict a Never Never Land of childhood where the world of 'faery' and the domestic world of nursery and garden intermingled with gentle harmony and sentiment.

Ida Rentoul Outhwaite was a perfect addition to this group. The fact that her fairy figures sometimes even combined the figures of the child and the angel only

'The Captain' by Ida Rentoul Outhwaite from FAIRYLAND.

served to strengthen the sense of a nursery religion in a developing graphic tradition. Increasingly, the Christian teaching from Victorian books was being replaced by fairy figures who imparted moral guidance to children. During the war years, Outhwaite's patriotic and religious sentiments had fused into visions of vulnerable adolescents with wing spans that were surely heaven sent! Whatever their genealogy, Outhwaite's figures contribute to this 1920s repertoire and were only usurped when the Second World War replaced them with characters from the animal world such as rabbits, teddy bears, dogs, horses and elephants.

Outhwaite's first venture into the competitive international market with A. & C. Black was *The Enchanted Forest* (1921). The limited edition presentation of her work in a cream cloth binding, meant to be reminiscent of vellum, was A. & C. Black's answer to the austere years just passed. Once again her timing was fortuitous: back in Australia the fantasy scene was being dominated by May Gibbs' more robust Australiana vision. *Fairyland* (1926) was Outhwaite's only major work to receive first publication in Australia in this decade. But her popularity at home was maintained by this near-companion to *Elves & Fairies,* her English printings and eight solo exhibitions.

With the reprinting of *Fairyland,* both in New York (1929) and London (1931), Ida Rentoul Outhwaite's great fairy books virtually came to an end. Thereafter there is a forcing of ideas and inspiration; a certain exuberance seems lost.

Many of her later illustrations depict a single figure or a few figures in stiffly posed, undramatic situations rather than in crowded and vital scenes. Her work gradually abandoned much of its fantasy element and tended to concentrate more on animals and children, frequently in an unadorned landscape. [9] The inevitable result was clearly pointed out by one critic in 1928: She [Outhwaite] is only appealing when she treats of fairies ... A be-crinolined little mortal sitting on the edge of a pond leaves one apathetic. [10]

Outhwaite's limited pictorial and technical vocabulary was no longer overlooked by critics sentimentalising in full-blown praise. In the aftermath of the First World War, much of the coinage of fantasy illustration looked bankrupt and the Depression finally turned the public towards a less romantic vision.

From the late 1930s to the late 1940s virtually the only outlet for Outhwaite's work was, distressingly, in the design of sheet music covers for the Melbourne publishers, Allan & Co. During the Second World War and just after, Australian children's illustrated books reached a low point in both quality of production and inspiration. With wartime restrictions on paper and imported printings, cheap local productions swamped the market. Garish and cute work trivialised much of the fantasy that had once been popular. The Melbourne firm of Murfetts introduced such second generation fantasy illustrators as Peg Maltby and Jean Elder, yet they could hardly sustain Australia's fantasy vision first begun by Ida Rentoul Outhwaite in 1903.

In an article that has previously eluded researchers, published on the eve of the Second World War, Outhwaite revealed her disappointment with the way the Australian publishing scene had collapsed:

The chief trouble of an Australian illustrator is that there is no work for him to do ... one publisher, who has produced a great many charming illustrated books, has pointed out that he has, most sorrowfully, been forced to give it up, or almost give it up. The cost of colour is high; the population of Australia small; the sale of enough copies to pay the price of publishing cannot be relied upon, and, in the case of children's books, it is impossible to compete against the showy, cheaply produced children's annuals from overseas, sold at a low price here, with which the market is flooded.[11]

Outhwaite's greatest achievement, perhaps, was in the establishment of children's book illustration in Australia as a popular and validated occupation. The marked success of her work in capturing the imagination of a large audience was the direct impetus behind the spate of finely produced and illustrated Australian children's fantasy books of the 1920s.

Today Outhwaite's work is enjoying a revival of interest as the vicissitudes of taste bring her name before the public again. In conclusion, I can only revert to an earlier summation which still does the evocative name of Ida Rentoul Outhwaite full justice:

She developed a unique fairyland vision which filled the Australian landscape with an engaging liaison between koalas, kangaroos, kookaburras, ethereal and lissom fairies, mischievous-looking elves and tidy, Edwardian children. In so doing she enriched the imagery and imaginative grasp of generations of young Australians as well as holding a worthy and deserved place in the golden age of British book illustration.[12]

ENDNOTES

1 'Sisters in art and letters,' *The Australian Book Buyer*, v.1 no.9, December 1912, p.221.

2 Ibid.

3 Ida Rentoul Outhwaite, 'Lesson 34: Developing the Imagination,' Melbourne: Art Training Institute, 1947?.

4 George Robertson of Melbourne (not to be confused with George Robertson of Sydney) began publishing in 1855, and his first book for children 'per se' was the third edition of *Bonwick's Geography of Australia and New Zealand* 1856.

5 Robert Holden, 'Painting, Publishing and Propaganda in 1916: The Genesis of the Australian Art Press,' in *The Art of F. McCubbin* Brisbane: Boolarong Publications, 1986.

6 [Review], *Bulletin*, 4 January 1917, 'Red Page.'

7 Colin White, *The World of the Nursery*, London: Herbert Press, 1984, p.80.

8 'Spartacus Smith', 'Catching Fairies in the Camera,' *Sydney Mail*, 19 January 1921, pp.10–11.

9 Marcie Muir & Robert Holden, *The Fairy World of Ida Rentoul Outhwaite*, Sydney: Craftsman Press, 1985, Chapter 13.

10 'Art Exhibitions: Miss [sic] Outhwaite's Pictures,' *Sydney Morning Herald*, 25 July 1928, p.17.

11 Ida Rentoul Outhwaite, 'The Troubles of an Australian Illustrator,' *Age* 'Literary Section,' 21 January 1939, p.9.

12 Marcie Muir & Robert Holden, Op.cit., p.153.

'My Little Son, Dandelion' by Ethel Jackson Morris from THE WHITE BUTTERFLY, *Melbourne, 1921.*

The 'Elves and Fairies' School

Visions of Fairyland

Sydney and Melbourne have flaunted their supposed differences since the nineteenth century. Melbourne has taunted Sydney with charges of 'empty show' while Sydney has retaliated by accusing Melbourne of 'stultifying propriety.' Marcus Clarke contributed to inter-colonial rivalry in 1887 by his characterisation of Melbourne as 'intellectual' and Sydney as 'fashionable and luxurious.'

This contrast and competition has also been fuelled by commentators on the Australian art scene who have declared that the artistic styles practised in each city are also polarised. Whatever truth there is in this claim, it is certainly an observable fact that the status and role of women artists in Melbourne were markedly different from that of their sisters in Sydney.

As early as 1882 an annual series of exhibitions by women artists was instituted in colonial Melbourne. Its practitioners were shown to be a positive force on the artistic scene. The single most significant fact was that the National Gallery School of Painting in Melbourne had, virtually since its inception in 1867, shown a marked preponderance of female students. These women were to become Australia's first generation of successful and professionally trained women artists, and the Australian Exhibition of Women's Work held in Melbourne in 1907 was the first major public statement of this generation's ability.

Together with such easel painters as Margaret Preston, Vida Lahey and Hilda Rix Nicholas, were other students whose talents and aspirations led them to choose less competitive modes of artistic expression, such as craft work, printmaking and illustration. In their day these professions were regarded as peripheral pursuits and helped enforce belittling stereotypes. Today, the contribution of these 'alternative' artists is being reassessed and evaluated.

One of the most notable exceptions to this

alternative fraternity in Melbourne was Ida Rentoul Outhwaite, a self-taught illustrator, who achieved a considerable solo exhibition profile, both locally and internationally. Her early success as a published illustrator (from 1903) was an inspiration and a challenge to many National Gallery School students who pursued the role of illustrator and graphic artist.

Foremost among these were Ethel Jackson Morris, Ethel Spowers, Christian Yandell and Edith Alsop. Although their final contribution to children's book illustration was individually small, when seen as a coherent artistic Melbourne phenomenon it becomes highly significant. This group, inspired by the example of Ida Rentoul Outhwaite, clearly constitute what can be called an 'Elves and Fairies' school of illustration.

Vignette illustration by Ethel Jackson Morris from THE WHITE BUTTERFLY.

At the start of their careers, Jackson Morris, Spowers, Yandell and Alsop were equally at home exhibiting with either the Victorian Artists' Society or the Arts & Crafts Society of Victoria. They saw themselves as moving freely between the world of academic art and that of the craftsperson. Their democratic attitude was indicative of a basic free-ranging approach to their art. However, one result of this attitude is the scattering of their efforts and documentation that is elusive and fragmentary.

Ethel Jackson Morris' career has remained unchronicled since the 1920s and most of her output remained stored away for more than 50 years, unseen and lost to posterity. Edith Alsop's most significant and large-scale work, which was for a children's hospital ward in 1910, was virtually forgotten by the 1930s and was not resurrected to public view until 1986. Ethel Spowers' career as a colour linocut artist totally overshadowed her earlier work in the Outhwaite tradition in the same way that Christian Yandell's popular profile as a stained-glass window designer and printmaker caused her earlier achievement as a fantasy artist to be forgotten.

The illustrative career of Ethel Jackson Morris (1891–1985) could serve as a paradigm for many other women artists of her generation: early dedication to academic training, initial exposure, lack of suitable commissions and opportunities commensurate with training and ability, disappointment and finally a retreat into a marriage, which brought an effective close to a once promising career. The reworking of this formula was a task many failed to negotiate; others broke away by virtue of family money, overseas exposure or sheer single mindedness.

Ethel Jackson Morris spent the year before she commenced her studies at the National Gallery School laboriously handwriting, illustrating and binding a number of fairy tales in a format and style identical to Ida Rentoul's own teenage works: *Mollie's Bunyip* (1904) and *Mollie's Staircase* (1906). Jackson Morris' first published work, *All Among the Fairies*, appeared in 1909 and was underwritten by her admiring father rather than issued as a clear commercial entity.

This fact alone serves to underline the dilettantish nature of Jackson Morris' initial achievement — like Alsop and Spowers she came from a prosperous Melbourne family, which could afford to indulge the artistic pursuits of its female members.

All Among the Fairies was a crudely executed and juvenile work. As an illustrative debut it gives virtually no indication of the sparkling talent that was to develop. It is significant only because it highlights by comparison the precocious ability of Ida Rentoul and the considerable influence she was to have on Jackson Morris and other aspiring fantasy illustrators in Melbourne.

In 1909 Jackson Morris visited London, an experience that widened her art horizon enormously. In her diary she records numerous visits to art galleries including, most significantly, a visit to the Leicester Galleries' exhibition of Edmund Dulac's 'Omar Khayyam' illustrations on 15 October 1909. Dulac was subsequently established as the major influence on her palette throughout the next decade.

It may seem extraordinary that between Jackson Morris' first appearance in print (1909) and the publication of her major illustrative work, *The White Butterfly* (1920), her fantasy vision did not find any substantial publishing outlet. In this decade Jackson Morris' only known publication *Mopsa the Fairy and Snowdrop and the Seven Dwarfs* (1916), was a very modest work, designed as a school reader. This minor publication, issued in wrappers, contains four full-page black and white illustrations and is hardly a challenge to Outhwaite's magnificent *Elves & Fairies* issued the same

Vignette illustration by Ethel Jackson Morris from THE WHITE BUTTERFLY.

Vignette illustration by Ethel Jackson Morris from THE WHITE BUTTERFLY.

'An Old Woman' by Ethel Jackson Morris from THE WHITE BUTTERFLY.

year. The only public exposure Jackson Morris had was the showing of nine fairy illustrations (including three from *Mopsa*) in the Victorian Artists' Society exhibition. [1]

Between 1910 and 1920, Ethel Jackson Morris' supportive family and secure economic standing enabled her to attend the National Gallery School. Her exhibiting career began in 1912 at the Victorian Artists' Society Annual Exhibition and the three watercolours shown, 'The Bat', 'Moon Fairy' and 'Nocturne' established her as a competent newcomer to the realms of fantasy illustration. Thereafter, and until 1920, she contributed to a further 11 such exhibitions.

Ethel Jackson Morris and her fellow Melbourne artists, unlike their counterparts on the Sydney scene, had the benefit of a State funded art teaching institution, which helped generate a sense of cultural identity. Furthermore, there were major exhibition opportunities for students to achieve public exposure: the National Gallery School held an annual exhibition of student's work and the Victorian Artists' Society held spring and annual exhibitions as well as specific genre exhibitions to which students were encouraged to submit.

Although Jackson Morris was only one student among many who exhibited with the Victorian Artists' Society, her work was usually singled out for praise in the critiques of the day. Early in 1916 her illustrations were seen to record 'a marked advance on anything ... previously shown'. [2] Later that year her pen work was described as 'remarkable for its completeness of execution and refined sense of composition'. [3]

Jackson Morris' exhibition profile stands in direct contrast to the Sydney experience. For example, May Gibbs who was the most professionally trained children's book illustrator on the Sydney scene never sought an exhibiting career and only contributed a very few works, mainly portraits, to the (Sydney) Society of Women Painters [4] while Dorothy Wall seems to have had only one solo exhibition. [5]

By the end of the decade the price of Jackson Morris' work had risen from 3 guineas to as much as 16 guineas and after leaving the Gallery School in 1920, she

Vignette illustration by Ethel Jackson Morris from THE WHITE BUTTERFLY.

announced her independence by holding a solo exhibition the next year. Seventy-five pen and ink and watercolour works were shown, including 28 from *The White Butterfly*, with prices ranging from 2 to 25 guineas. With this book, written and illustrated by Jackson Morris, she laid the promise of being a serious rival to Ida Rentoul Outhwaite. It was launched at an exhibition in Fine Arts Society's galleries in November 1921.

Alexander Colquhoun offered an evaluation of this exhibition:

This artist appears to have developed a settled, even quality of work, which admits of little in the way of innovation and spontaneity, while the technical cleverness of line, and general arrangement of colour, though attractive, is in a measure stereotyped. The drawings are, for the most part, illustrations of fairy lore, or kindred matter, treated from the decorative rather than the imaginative point of view, and what they lack in humour is made up for by a certain piquant quaintness which is one of their most assertive features.

Miss Morris understands how to dispose of masses of solid black with line and colour in such a way as to produce an easy sense of balance and composition, while her drawing is invariably carefully studied, even to the detail of hands and feet, lacking only in general, that rare quality of inspiration, to raise it from the stage of cleverness to a more distinguished level. [6]

Colquhoun's criticism that the work was treated from a 'decorative' rather than an 'imaginative' point of view and his closing remark on inspiration could be applied to the whole school of fantasy illustration as it existed in Australia at the time. Outhwaite, certainly a more imaginative fantasy illustrator than Jackson Morris, was to suffer the same judgment, albeit later in her career. It is, in fact, surprising that Colquhoun did not compare these women artists in his review: Outhwaite had shown in the same galleries less than 6 months before. Another reviewer of Jackson Morris' exhibition also failed to mention Outhwaite as a fellow fantasy illustrator. [7] It seems strange and uninformed that no-one saw a coherent school of fantasy illustration developing in Melbourne at the time.

But Jackson Morris' triumph was short-lived. Although she had a fine publication to her credit, the book failed to attract the acclaim Outhwaite was receiving. Jackson Morris deserted her home town and returned briefly to London.

Outhwaite's domination of the illustrative scene, her superior talent and the guiding business hand and acumen of her husband, hardly left room in the small world of Australian children's book publishing for another fantasy illustrator in the same 'Elves and Fairies' vein. Most of the original work from *The White Butterfly* remained unsold and probably the last Melbourne exhibition that Morris contributed to was the Annual Exhibition of the Arts & Crafts Society of Victoria later that month.

The following year Jackson Morris travelled to London where she enrolled in classes in etching and engraving at the Royal College of Art. In 1923 she returned to Australia and settled in Sydney. She exhibited once with the (Sydney) Society of Artists in the Annual Exhibition of 1929

'Came dancing toward her, two Beautiful Fairies' by Ethel Jackson Morris from THE WHITE BUTTERFLY.

'If I sing well enough' by Ethel Spowers from A*RROWS OF* L*ONGING, Melbourne, 1921.*

and married the next year. Thereafter she withdrew from the art world entirely and her illustrative career came to an end. Australia had lost one of its most promising fantasy artists.

Ethel Jackson Morris' work, particularly that in black and white, has a clarity and a sense of design which does not rely on dazzling ornamentation for its effect. Jackson Morris' sparseness provides a contrasting foil to Outhwaite's work, and her accomplished use of watercolour was used for greater atmospheric effect. *The White Butterfly*, an undeservedly forgotten book today, must surely rank as one of the most beautifully produced and illustrated children's books in the whole fairy genre in Australia.

Both Ethel Jackson Morris and Ida Rentoul Outhwaite were keenly aware of contemporary fantasy illustration on the international scene. They attempted to follow in the current international vogue for deluxe editions and worked almost exclusively in an English style with little Australian reference.

Outhwaite's observable debt to Charles and Heath Robinson's pen and ink work has already been noted [8]; Jackson Morris, by contrast, drew on the influence of colourists, in particular Edmund Dulac and Kay Nielsen. Her predilection for luminous blues, greens and purples is taken directly from Dulac's palette while some of her simpler pen and ink work shows a debt to Nielsen's Nordic sense of composition and design.

Arthur Rackham was a ubiquitous influence and inspiration for most fantasy illustrators, whether in Australia or elsewhere, and Ethel Jackson Morris' depiction of clutching, menacing trees is certainly derived from his example. Unlike Rackham, however, Jackson Morris never explored the grotesque possibilities of the fairy realm. She chose to depict a gentler fantasy world; the 'darker' side of fantasy illustration is only momentarily glimpsed in the work of fellow illustrators Harold Gaze and Minnie Rowe.

Among Jackson Morris' contemporaries there were others who played a significant part in the establishment of a Melbourne school of fantasy illustration. These include Edith Alsop and Christian Yandell, who were also strongly influenced by fellow practitioners on the international scene. Alsop's early and two-dimensional approach is derived from Walter Crane's 'toybook' style, while Yandell's pen and ink work in the Art Nouveau revival style owes a considerable debt to the Irishman Harry Clarke.

This emulation of an imported pictorial tradition was more characteristic of Melbourne than Sydney. Children's book illustrators in Melbourne drew freely on a validated pictorial vocabulary and at least in the case of Ethel Jackson Morris and Ida Rentoul Outhwaite they made a significant local contribution to that vocabulary.

Another figure in this clique of fantasy illustrators was Ethel Spowers, a particularly close friend of Ethel Jackson Morris. It is appropriate that her early career should be considered in conjunction with that of her namesake.

'Children on a Flying Horse' by Ethel Spowers.

Ever since the mid-1970s, Australian 'modernist' printmakers have enjoyed an overdue reappraisal and their achievement has been celebrated in exhibitions and documented in catalogues, surveys and monographs. One of those to emerge as a foremost practitioner in this area has been Ethel Spowers (1880–1947). Her connection with Claude Flight and the Grosvenor School of Art (London) has resulted in both international as well as local reappraisal.

Spowers' style and approach to colour linocutting were significantly changed by her contact, at the end of 1928 and again in 1931, with the teachings of the Grosvenor School. Back in Australia, Spowers acted as agent and publicist for Claude Flight and his circle, and for a decade was a popular exhibitor of decorative colour linocuts. While no-one would disagree that her major achievement lies in this field, today's reappraisal has tended to dismiss or even neglect her earlier profile as a fantasy artist. Commentators either see her work as worthy of attention only in its post-Flight stage or dismiss her earlier work with a few cursory lines:

Ethel Spowers' style changed markedly as a result of Flight's tuition. From the mid-1920s Spowers had attained moderate success in Melbourne working as a decorative illustrator of nursery tales in a variety of media, including linocut. [9]

Spowers' early work, going back as far as her student days, deserves more consideration. Her later achievements can more sensibly be set within a meaningful context only when this coherent earlier period is assessed. While there was certainly a marked change in her style and subject matter after 1928, two major constants remained: a continuing interest in the illustrative incident, and an on-going regard for decorative appeal.

These abiding interests are clearly part of Spowers' legacy from her early involvement in arts and crafts pursuits. She came from a wealthy and socially prominent family with a share in two major newspapers. Unlike

'Hansel and Gretel' by Ethel Spowers.

the Sydney scene which seemed to be energised by lone figures, such as May Gibbs and Dorothy Wall, Melbourne seemed to encourage and generate family involvement in a host of intellectual and cultural pursuits. The Spowers' family joined others such as the Alsops and the Rentouls in an extended contribution to Melbourne's cultural scene.

Certainly the Spowers' girls were all encouraged to take up arts and crafts pursuits and while her sisters became adept at bookbinding and needlework, Ethel developed her illustrative talent. In 1905, at the age of 15, two of her fairy drawings

'Children in a Tree' by Ethel Spowers.

'Card playing by moonlight' by Ethel Spowers.

were reproduced in the *Australian.* [10] This precocious achievement paralleled Ida Rentoul's first appearance in print at fifteen. [11]

Spowers' interest in fantasy illustration was encouraged and maintained in her student work at the National Gallery School where she studied between 1911 and 1917 and met Ethel Jackson Morris. The close supportive friendship and shared vision of these two during their formative years has never been documented or assessed, yet their lives ran parallel courses for many years.

They were born within a year of each other, trained together at the Gallery School, exhibited in the same student and Victorian Artists' Society exhibitions, launched their solo careers at exhibitions that were almost complementary, produced their first major illustrated books in 1921 and were both in London in 1922 pursuing new interests in printmaking. Thereafter, however, Jackson Morris was disappointed with the reception of her fantasy work and the lack of illustrative commissions. Perhaps she convinced Spowers of the need to concentrate more on her printmaking activities and eventually replace fantasy with subjects more attuned to daily life.

Certainly Spowers herself was never given the opportunity to display her fantasy work in any really suitable publication. *Arrows of Longing* (Melbourne: Alexander McCubbin, 1921), a volume of poetry by 'Furnley Maurice', could hardly be considered a showpiece for Spowers' talent. Its stiff and

'The Witch Dance' by Ethel Jackson Morris.

awkward figures have little of the decorative appeal we usually associate with her work, and the publication is an uneasy alliance between a poetry book and a limited edition art book.

Ethel Spowers' contributions to Victorian Artists' Society exhibitions in the years leading up to 1920 were usually inspired by fairy tales and episodes drawn from the literature of myth and fable. In 1916 she exhibited 'Red Riding Hood', in 1918 a series of illustrations to Hans Christian Andersen stories and in 1919 such works as 'The Witch in her Garden' and 'The Magic Wood'. This thematic emphasis was maintained in her first solo exhibition held at Melbourne's Decoration Galleries in June 1920. The 30 watercolours included an 'Illustration to the Frog Prince', two illustrations to Grimm's tale of 'The Twelve Brothers', an illustration to 'Isabella and the Pot of Basil' and others with fantasy themes. The 22 black and white works included 'The Sorceress', 'The Changeling', 'The Naiad', and a work lent by Ethel Jackson Morris. The whole appeal of the exhibition was succinctly conveyed in the *Argus'* review:

> *The appeal of fairy lore and of old romance is strongly felt and well expressed. In many of the designs the impression is given of a world in which strange events are soon to happen. Suggestion is conveyed of the hush of enchanted forests, and of mystery that the wayfarer will find beyond the hilltop.* [12]

Such a summation could be applied to the whole Melbourne school of 'Elves and Fairies' illustration.

The following year (1921) Spowers was in London where she held a joint exhibition with fellow Australian Mary Reynolds. After four years in London and Paris she returned to Melbourne and eventually reintroduced herself to the public with another successful solo exhibition. Together with appearances in Arts & Crafts [13] and other group exhibitions, she then began to introduce prints into her exhibiting repertoire. In August 1925 her second solo exhibition in Melbourne was described thus:

> *There have been many artists for the most part women, whose contribution to art takes the form of illustrating fairy stories, children's games and poster designs in black and white and colour. In this direction, Miss Ethel Spowers undisputedly holds pride of place ...* [14]

Both of the major reviews of this exhibition singled out a suite of illustrations to 'Cinderella' for particular praise and one critic called them 'the best fairy drawings we have seen'. [15]

At her first exhibition in Sydney the following year, a series of 'Cinderella' illustrations in woodcut were similarly praised, although another developing facet of her work was also noticed — her sympathetic depiction of children and childhood. [16] Her final exhibition before leaving for London again and establishing an initial contact with modernist printmakers was in August 1927. Right up to the evening of departure she reaffirmed this new direction in her work as she moved from fantasy to decorative studies like 'Children in a Tree'.

The result of this confirmed interest in children as subjects led to her being

'The Noisy Parrot' by Ethel Spowers.

characterised as 'the nursery artist' the next month in Melbourne's leading women's magazine. [17] Although Spowers had first begun printmaking (black and white woodcuts) c. 1923 and linocutting soon afterwards, her reputation before 1928 was obviously as an illustrator of fantasy and childhood themes. Of the few prints from this early period that have survived, most utilise these themes and none more charmingly than the colour linocut of 'The Noisy Parrot' (1926)' which must be her masterpiece in this medium before the influence of modernist teachings.

The elusive record of exhibition catalogues proves that Ethel Spowers and Ethel Jackson Morris produced a significant volume of fantasy work. The fact that most of it was never preserved in print or that the originals have largely disappeared from view make an assessment of their worth difficult. However, the few illustrations gathered here are enough to reveal a strength of vision and a valid contribution to a coherent Melbourne phenomenon — the 'Elves and Fairies' school of illustration.

ENDNOTES

1 V. A. S. Watercolour & Black and White Exhibition, September 1916.

2 A. Colquhoun, 'Victorian Artists ...', *Herald*, 9 May 1916, p.l.

3 A. Colquhoun, 'Victorian Art ...', *Herald*, 23 September 1916, p.16.

4 See their Annual Exhibitions 1922–1924 and their Exhibition of Cabinet Pictures & Craft Work, 1921.

5 Exhibition in H. C. Swain's Gallery, May 1927.

6 A. Colquhoun, 'Water Colour & Pen Work ...', *Herald*, 7 November 1921, p.7.

7 *Argus*, 8 November 1921, p.10.

8 See Marcie Muir & Robert Holden, *The Fairy World of Ida Rentoul Outhwaite* Sydney, Craftsman Press, 1985, p.150.

9 Stephen Coppel, 'Claude Flight and his Australian Pupils', *Print Quarterly*, v.2 no. 4, December 1985, p.277.

10 Roger Butler, 'Electricity Castle', in *Creating Australia*, edited by Daniel Thomas, Art Gallery South Australia, Adelaide 1988, p.172.

11 See *The New Idea*, August–December 1903.

12 Art Exhibitions...', *Argus* 22 June 1920, p.7.

13 See Arts & Crafts Society of Victoria Exhibition, September 1925 in which she exhibited woodcuts in company with Evelyn Syme.

14 Art Notes ...', *Age*, 4 August 1925, p.9.

15 Ibid.

16 See 'Art Exhibition ...', *Sydney Morning Herald*, 1 June 1926, p.10.

17 *Women's World*, September 1927, p.493.

'On a fish's back astride ...' by Edith Alsop from SOME CHILDREN'S SONGS, *Melbourne, 1910.*

A Melbourne Quartet

Edith Alsop, Christian Yandell, Harold Gaze, Minnie Rowe

The friendship and shared artistic vision between Ethel Jackson Morris and Ethel Spowers were generated within a distinct Melbourne clique where social standing as well as artistic temperament were factors in common. This social milieu, rather different to the more independent lifestyle that fostered the careers of May Gibbs and Dorothy Wall on the Sydney scene, meant that Ethel Jackson Morris and the five Spowers sisters were able to share imaginative space with the Alsop sisters, Christian Yandell, Betty and Esther Paterson, Ola Cohn and others.

In particular, Edith Alsop and Christian Yandell were contemporary associates of Jackson Morris and Spowers who contributed to the establishment of a Melbourne 'Elves and Fairies' school of fantasy illustration, and their efforts warrant extended consideration. The work of Harold Gaze and Minnie Rowe lies outside this Melbourne clique and provides a contrast to its somewhat incestuous style. Their less derivative fantasy style shows the imaginative coherence of Jackson Morris and company, who promoted a gentler 'more English' vision.

Between 1898 and 1905, Edith Alsop was a student at the National Gallery School of Painting in Melbourne and a regular contributor to Victorian Artists' Society exhibitions between 1903 and 1926. She was born into a gifted and prominent Melbourne family in 1871 and after her initial art training achieved a local profile as a graphic artist and illustrator of children's books. Although she was hardly a prolific children's book illustrator, the quality of her work is such that Marcie Muir lamented: 'An opportunity seems to have been missed when an artist such as Edith Alsop of Melbourne illustrated only two children's books'. [1]

'Mary, Mary, Quite Contrary' by Ida Rentoul Outhwaite, 1910.

'This is the Way we Wash our Hands' by Edith Alsop, 1910.

Alsop later broke away from her limited sphere of artistic expression and developed a more cosmopolitan and independent vision after various European trips, which introduced her to modernist influences in the art world. She studied wood-engraving at the Central School of Arts & Crafts in London and painting in Paris under Andre Lhote. On her return to Melbourne, she enrolled in George Bell's painting classes. She remained in the forefront of art movements and became a founding member of both the Contemporary Art Group and the Independent Group of Artists when she was in her early sixties.

Edith Alsop's early interest in fantasy illustration was first brought into public prominence in July 1910 when, together with Ida Rentoul Outhwaite, Janet Cumbrae-Stewart and' Jessie Traill, she provided a series of large-scale nursery rhyme panels to decorate two children's wards in Melbourne's Homoeopathic Hospital.[2] Edith's work in these panels is remarkably complementary to that of Ida Rentoul Outhwaite. Its poster-like effects are achieved by bold lettering, hieratic foreground figures and pictorial repetition. Edith had, in fact, submitted a poster design to the 1907 Exhibition of Women's Work and her eight panels of nursery rhymes are composed in the same mode.

Alsop and Outhwaite produced their fantasy panels in one ward as a complement to the more realistic work by the other artists, which depicted children's games and pastimes. There is evidence that these two collaborated imaginatively on at least one pair of panels. By 1910, Ida Rentoul Outhwaite had evolved a distinct and personal pictorial vocabulary, which is clearly in evidence in three of the four panels that are extant today. (It is unfortunate that not all the hospital panels have survived or been located.) Outhwaite's only nursery rhyme panel, 'Mary, Mary, Quite Contrary' uses less of her personal style and shows more the influence of Kate Greenaway. In this way it is almost a twin of

'We fell through the stars' by Edith Alsop from THE COBWEB LADDER*, Melbourne, 1916.*

'A perfectly scrumptious watermelon' by Christian Yandell from THE ADVENTUROUS ELVES*, Melbourne, 1926.*

Alsop's, 'This is the Way we Wash our Hands'. Later in 1910, Alsop's illustrations appeared in *Some Children's Songs.* This volume confirmed her as a competent illustrator working in the flat, two-dimensional style of decorative work derived from English children's book illustration, especially that of Walter Crane, whose work would have been popular in the Alsop nursery.

Edith Alsop's lavish production was most likely inspired by Ida Rentoul Outhwaite's series of songbooks (1907–1913) in which the second volume, *Bush Songs of Australia,* coincidentally appeared in 1910. Annie Rentoul provided the words in this series and, similarly, Marion Alsop contributed her design skills to her sister's volume. The result was a much more ambitious production than the Outhwaite series: its five large colour plates, generous borders, decorative vignettes and calligraphy all combine harmoniously. A hardcover limited edition was also issued, quite likely subsidised by the authors themselves.

Throughout the next few years Edith's energy was mainly expended on providing work for magazine covers and she seemed destined to achieve no more than minor commissions. However, in September 1916, Lothians published *The Cobweb Ladder* with 7 of her full-page black and white fantasy illustrations. [3] This children's book, written by Joice Nankivell, has the distinction of appearing the month before Outhwaite's *Elves & Fairies* was itself published by Lothians. However, *The Cobweb Ladder* was overshadowed by the much greater impact of Outhwaite's book. Lothian's later wrote to Ida confirming the primacy of her vision:

> *We know Mrs Outhwaite is very busy, but we are wondering if it could be arranged for a book to be published in style similar to* The Cobweb Ladder, *containing poems by Miss Rentoul, with pictures by Mrs Outhwaite.* [4]

Vignette illustration by Christian Yandell from THE GATES OF DAWN.

Elves & Fairies was validated by a list of vice-regal and noted subscribers and once it was launched, Outhwaite's sellout exhibitions became prominent social occasions. There seemed little room for lesser talents in the same vein or for those with only moderate ambition and motivation. Faced with this formidable competition, Edith Alsop, like Ethel Jackson Morris a few years later, turned away from her developing profile as a children's book illustrator. Her final commission in this genre would appear to be *Tales of the Fairies,* a very minor effort for Whitcombe & Tombs in the 1920s.

'The Witch and the Giant' by Christian Yandell from THE GATES OF DAWN.

Another fantasy illustrator who played a part in the establishment of an 'Elves and Fairies' fantasy vision was Christian Yandell (1895–1956). She also studied at the National Gallery School of Painting (between 1909 and 1914), where she met her future husband Napier Waller. The artistic stimulus of this marriage resulted in a memorable collaboration in printmaking, stained glass window design, mural design and mosaic work.

Christian Yandell's principal activity in the decade after the First World War was fantasy illustration; some of these works were exhibition pieces, others were for specifically commissioned books. In May 1919, for example, she contributed a number of illustrations to the Victorian Artists' Society annual exhibition, such as 'The Spirit of the Desolate Wood' and 'The Gateway to Nowhere'. Thereafter she provided illustrations for such children's books as Lewis Carroll's *Alice in Wonderland* (1924), Hume Cook's *Australian Fairy Tales* (1925) and May Paten's *The Adventurous Elves* (1926). *Australian Fairy Tales*, with its six colour plates and 11 full-page black and white illustrations is the major work among these titles.

In the following decades, Christian Yandell tended to concentrate increasingly on stained glass window design, printmaking and mystical studies, which inspired and infused her imagery and expression. The marked preference she had shown since her early years for artistic subjects drawn from myth and legend was maintained in an adult search for a catholic vocabulary that utilised symbolism, astrology and numerology.

The refining of Christian Yandell's unique pictorial vision throughout the 1930s was influenced by a number of artistic elements: Art Deco; the book illustrations of Harry Clarke, whose stained glass studios in Dublin she visited; the Vienna Secessionist style; and the increasing influence of stained glass window design. The latter is shown in the strong vertical lines and the hypnotic swirls and sunbursts of decorative detail that keep the eye in motion over her whole picture plane. This style was used to great effect in the early 1930s in a children's book, *The Gates of Dawn*, which she hoped to publish through her own Golden Arrow Press. Unfortunately, only one copy of these pen and ink illustrations with hand written text was printed (by lithography) and it was not until 1977 that a more accessible edition was printed by Gryphon Books.

Vignette illustration by Harold Gaze from THE CHEWG-UM-BLEWG-UM, *Melbourne, 1919.*

When viewed in conjunction with similar work by Ida Rentoul Outhwaite, the illustrations of Ethel Jackson Morris, Ethel Spowers, Edith Alsop and Christian Yandell show the existence of a coherent school of illustrators inspired by fairytale, myth and fantasy. These illustrators saw themselves as working within a fine art tradition and imported their pictorial vocabulary from English book illustration of the day. Their Sydney counterparts, on the other hand, were more likely to find inspiration in the Australian environment and experience, and to develop a more original, robust and boisterous pictorial vocabulary, which included Gumnut Babies, Banksia Men and Blinky Bill.

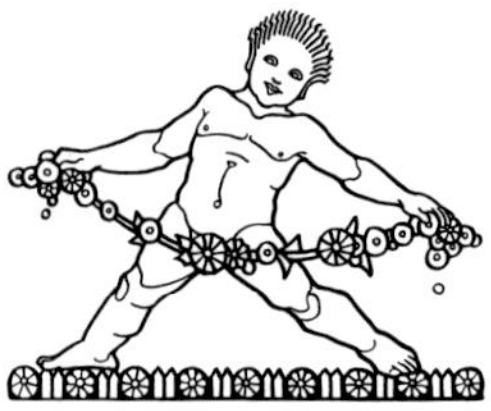

Vignette illustration by Christian Yandell from THE GATES OF DAWN, *Sydney, 1977.*

New Zealand's best known illustrator/author of children's books was Dorothy Wall, who was born in 1894 and emigrated to Australia in 1914. Since then Desmond Digby (b.1933), Pamela Allen (b.1934), Bruce Treloar (b.1946), Deborah and Kilmeny Niland (b.1952) and Rodney McRae (b.1958) have also braved the Tasman Sea and enriched Australian children's literature. Yet before these figures were even born there was an outstanding fantasy illustrator whose peripatetic life may have confused many as to his true country of origin. This illustrator was Harold Gaze who was born in New Zealand in 1885 and died in California in 1962.

Between 1918 and 1921, Harold Gaze wrote and illustrated nine fantasy works for children, all but two of which were published in Melbourne. Unfortunately, there is a dearth of information about his background and training so that he appears to descend at the peak of his powers on the flourishing fantasy clique in Melbourne. Even in this august company, the quality and distinctive style of Gaze's work singled him out as an important newcomer certain to make an individual contribution to the fantasy genre.

Gaze reputedly studied for a short period at various art schools in London during the early years of the First World War. Although it is quite likely that Gaze would have contributed illustrations to books and magazines while in England, the first title we know of is actually an American imprint, *If I Could Fly* by Rose Strong Hubbell (1917). This little-known work contains five full-page colour illustrations, but unfortunately the quality of reproduction is insufficient to convey the finesse and delicacy of Gaze's watercolours. The frontispiece for this book was exhibited in the Victorian Artists' Society Annual Exhibition in May 1919.

Harold Gaze presumably arrived in Australia just before the end of the war in time to arrange for the Christmas issue of his first Australian title, *The Wicked Winkapong*. In September the following year he contributed one illustration from this book to a Victorian Artists' Society Water-colour & Cabinet Picture exhibition and a new talent was effectively launched on the Australian scene.

1919 was an extremely productive year and four new titles written and illustrated by Harold Gaze appeared: *The Billibonga Bird, The Chewg-um-blewg-um, The Simple Jaggajay* and *Coppertop*. The first three works are a trilogy of interrelated verse narratives and are surely the most lavish children's books ever issued by Whitcombe & Tombs, more usually known for modest works in an unpretentious house style.

By Australian standards these titles were milestones in the history of children's book production. Their large quarto format, with a colour illustration pasted to the front wrapper and the pleasing typography and layout were indicative of the publisher's understandable enthusiasm and belief that a major new talent had arrived. Only the year before, Whitcombe & Tombs had published another significant series — the six booklets that comprise the 'Willie Winkie Zoo Books.' This earlier series had been illustrated by Ida Rentoul Outhwaite

THE BILLIBONGA BIRD

By HAROLD GAZE

The Mite Merry Series

and the much enlarged format of Gaze's trilogy in the 'Mite Merry Series' showed off his talent to greater advantage.

The six coloured and three black and white full-page illustrations are dated 1919. Considering the fact that Gaze preferred to work to a scale suitable for exhibition purposes, this was a most prolific year indeed. It is possible that he was an extremely fast worker. It is also possible that he arrived in Melbourne with an impressive portfolio of finished watercolours and accompanying texts with which to impress and tempt local publishers. The latter is clearly the case with *War in Fairyland.* It was listed on the title page of *Coppertop* in 1919 but was not actually published until 1921 and a close look at the illustrations reveals that the colour plates are signed and dated 1910! Even without knowledge of this anomaly, these illustrations seem considerably less assured than those produced later in the decade.

It is possible that Gaze made a brief return trip to New Zealand about this time, for *The China Cat* and *The Enchanted Fish,* two small booklets written and illustrated by him, were published in Auckland. In the early 1920s he resided briefly in Sydney where the original model for *Coppertop* lived. Harold Gaze then moved to London where at least six titles with his illustrations appeared between 1924 and 1931: *Coppertop* (1924, a combined edition of the earlier work together with its sequel, *Coppertop Cruises*); *The Goblin's Glen* (1924), *Last Fairy Tales* (1924); *The Merry Piper* (1925); *Tales of a Little Brown Man* (1925) and *The Wonder World Fairy Tale Book* (1931). Some of these titles also appeared in American editions and it is possible that their success encouraged Gaze to settle in that country permanently.

In 1927 he moved to Pasadena and lived there until his death in 1962. In the 1930s he held a number of successful solo exhibitions in Los Angeles where his fantasy illustrations earned him the title 'The Bubble Man'. Increasingly his works tended to highlight the unclad charms of his female fantasy figures and in this respect they moved away from their former appeal to a young audience and courted more adult appreciation.

Gaze's work in Australia between 1918 and 1921 established him as the most original illustrator of children's books after Ida Rentoul Outhwaite. Following D. H. Souter, he was the first male illustrator to enter a field dominated by women and produce a substantial volume of fantasy work. His illustrations are characterised by opalescent hues and are akin to those of Charles Folkard (the English illustrator) in their marked delight in the bizarre possibilities of the fairy realm. Both Gaze's text and illustrations are marked by an exuberance, and a wilfully extravagant imagination. He could be likened to Lewis Carroll in his vision of a wonderland peopled by the bizarre as well as by the beautiful.

Like Arthur Rackham, Gaze frequently introduced anthropomorphic touches into his work, with trees, waves and rocks taking on human features. Apart from his delightful use of silhouette (unfortunately not used often enough), Gaze's forte was

'The Foundling Fairy' by Harold Gaze.

obviously in watercolour. In this medium his work stands pre-eminent in the whole field of fantasy illustration in Australian children's books.

In comparing his technical expertise in this area with examples by Ida Rentoul Outhwaite, we can immediately see just how much of her colour work is primarily pen and ink drawing with only an added embellishment of colour. Harold Gaze, however, conceived his illustrations as colour entities from the beginning and it is regrettable that inferior printings failed to convey their subtlety and luminosity.

The last significant fantasy illustrator in Melbourne to contribute to the 'Elves and Fairies' genre at this time was Minnie Rowe. She is an elusive and hitherto undocumented author/illustrator whose three books, *The Wand of Dawn* (1918), *Gully Folk* (1919) and *Nancy in the Bush* (1923), contribute a naive note to the genre.

Minnie Isabella Rowe, who sometimes signed her work 'Miro', was born on 13 April 1882 in Adelong, Victoria. She was one of six surviving children born to Richard Harry Rowe and Thomasina Rodda. No doubt her remote country upbringing and complete lack of formal art training account for the strange and naive quality to her work. Her fantasy creations have a kind of elemental charm, although there is always a strong link with the closely observed world of nature.

Minnie Rowe was a highly regarded and much loved teacher, dedicated to her profession. A didactic purpose lies behind her writing motivated by her desire to inform as well as delight a young audience in the world of the Australian bush.

Her slightly nightmarish and surreal illustrations are unique in the Australian fantasy tradition although, at times, their grotesquerie evokes Harold Gaze's early efforts in that direction. Her illustrations seem to owe more to English fantasy illustrators of the nineteenth century, such as E. V. Boyle and Richard Doyle, than to any Australian contemporaries.

Minnie Rowe moved to Melbourne before the First World War where she continued teaching, most notably at the Fitzroy Domestic Arts School. She never seems to have exhibited or become a member of an art group there, although she did befriend such artists as Ola Cohn, Margaret Mahood and, significantly, Harold Gaze. Perhaps her only published contribution to the teaching profession is Whitcombe & Tombs *Vivid History Readers*, which she illustrated for Victorian Elementary Schools in the 1920s.

Edith Alsop, Christian Yandell, Harold Gaze and Minnie Rowe made a small yet coherent contribution to the 'Elves and Fairies' school of fantasy illustration in Melbourne earlier this century. For some, like Edith Alsop, their small volume of known work is of most significance when seen in comparison with that of Ida Rentoul Outhwaite. For others, Harold Gaze in particular, there is a quality of work which singles it out as distinctive and original.

ENDNOTES

1 Marcie Muir, *A History of Australian Children's Book Illustration*, Melbourne: O.U.P., 1982, p.75.

2 See Robert Holden, *Cheer up Children* [Exhibition Catalogue], Melbourne: Prince Henry's Hospital, 1986.

3 Two illustrations from *The Cobweb Ladder* were exhibited in the V.A.S. Annual Exhibition, May 1917.

4 Letter to Grenbry Outhwaite, 27 July 1917, Lothian Papers, State Library of Victoria.

'Meg and Nodrog pass a Sentry' by Minnie Rowe from THE WAND OF DAWN*, Melbourne, 1918.*

'The Art Gallery' by May Gibbs from S*NUGGLEPOT AND* C*UDDLEPIE, Sydney, 1918.*

May Gibbs

Creator of a National Pictorial Mythology

The Australian bush has always been a place of wonder and mystery. The Aborigines peopled it with mythic creations from the Dreamtime, and creatures such as the bunyip worked their spell upon the early white settlers. By the end of the nineteenth century when scientific as well as romantic documentation of Australia's natural environment had reached new heights, the Australian bush was considered much less alien territory. While botanical artists were meticulously depicting the native flora, the Heidelberg School was establishing its archetypal vision of eternal golden summers. In purely imaginative terms, however, one artist established our first popular visual mythology.

With her bushland babies May Gibbs created white Australia's first major pictorial folklore; they are part of an almost organic derivation from the Australian bush, the best known and most evocative after the Heidelberg School. Only the fact of its juvenile appeal has hindered a full acknowledgment of its national status. May Gibbs truly laid the foundation of a new Australian folklore.

Cecilia May Gibbs (1877–1969) was born in Kent, England, and emigrated to South Australia with her parents and two brothers in 1881. After a brief stay there the family finally settled in Western Australia, just south of Perth. Gibbs' parents had both attended art school in London and her father soon found employment in Perth as master at Perth High School. From 1891 until his retirement in 1917, he worked as a clerk for the Lands and Survey Department. Both parents were active in the literary and artistic life of Perth and encouraged Gibbs' early interest in drawing and illustrating. By the time she was 12, she had had a full-page of vignette illustrations published in the *West*

'The Society of Gumnut Artists' by May Gibbs from L*ITTLE* R*AGGED* B*LOSSOM, Sydney, 1920.*

Australian Bulletin (1889). This precocious talent was given a solid academic base in the first decade of this century when she studied in London art schools.

The most renowned Australian woman artist in these days, both locally and internationally, was the botanical artist Ellis Rowan. When this artist held a solo exhibition in Perth in 1907, May Gibbs, who was back home between her second and last overseas study trips, was immediately inspired to produce her own large botanical works. Gibbs was still searching for her own artistic niche. Her intense and short-lived dedication to natural history was later to stand her in good stead when this acute observation of the Australian bush anchored her fantasy illustrations with just the right proportion of reality.

Gibbs' third and final period of studies in London turned her towards caricature and cartoon work and children's book illustration. Between 1909 and 1912 she began to establish a name for herself as an illustrator. Her first major work, *About Us*, published in London in 1912, was inspired by an urban vision. Although it is a fantasy there is not a gumnut baby anywhere in sight — the work, written and illustrated by Gibbs, is set on the London rooftops.

Unfortunately, the English climate began to affect her health and Gibbs was forced to return to Sydney just before the First World War. She came back with much experience as a regular contributor to newspapers, magazines and books. In 1913, independent of family at last, Gibbs was able to establish her own lifestyle. In canvassing the local press and publishers for commissions, May Gibbs could easily have fulfilled the promise of her academic training and become a fine portraitist or miniaturist. Certainly she could have established an exhibition profile, both in groups such as the Society of Artists or the Society of Women Painters, and independently in one-woman exhibitions.

But fantasy illustration was becoming her forte and when she returned to the inspiration of her childhood upbringing in the Australian bush a unique artistic vision flourished at last. The way she found her niche in the art world was as serendipitous as it was timely. Soon after her arrival in Sydney, May Gibbs was asked to design a bookmark.

Someone asked me to make them a bookmark and I designed one with a gumleaf and two funny little animals peeping over the top. Out of the two funny little animals were born Bib and Bub, the gumnut babies, and since then I have never looked back. [1]

From this small beginning she became the first full-time, professionally trained children's book illustrator in Australia.

First World War postcard by May Gibbs.

The Roycroft Library (Sydney) promoted these hand-painted bookmarks and sold them at five shillings each. The demand for them, however, was so great that soon they were being printed and sold at sixpence each. Copyright registration was taken out late in 1913 and thereafter the gumnut babies entered Australian folklore.

Among Gibbs' numerous magazine commissions at this time, her three covers for the *Lone Hand* were specially significant. The first of these, in January 1914, featured the gumnut babies timidly peeping over a camouflage of gum leaves. The launching of such imagery could not have been better timed. The emerging war effort was federating a country which had, perhaps, never before been so unified. A national and heartfelt sentiment sought expression in patriotic symbols and images.

Thereafter her work was popularised at an astonishing rate, first as postcards and calendars and then as a series of five booklets (*Gumnut Babies, Gum Blossom Babies, Flannel Flower Babies, Boronia Babies, Wattle Babies*) that carried her work throughout the world. Today these booklets are generally regarded as children's items, but in their day they were issued in individual envelopes and were intended to be used as enlarged greeting cards. They were expanded versions of some of the dramatic little incidents depicted on her postcards.

Besides the gumnut babies, her postcards frequently featured a kookaburra, which appeared in many wartime situations either on the homefront as a kindly mother knitting for the troops, or as a soldier decked out in a slouch hat. As one contemporary report noted:

'Mr Lizard sat in his little Balcony' by May Gibbs from NUTTYBUB AND NITTERSING, *Melbourne, 1923.*

'At the Seaside' by May Gibbs from LITTLE RAGGED BLOSSOM.

Though the Nuts are friends with all the Bush folk and love all the world, they are just a little afraid of lizards and snakes; but even the wickedest snake wouldn't hurt a Nut.

Double-page spread from GUMNUT BABIES *by May Gibbs, Sydney, 1916.*

In thousands every week now, the whimsical cards and other art productions from Miss Gibbs' prolific brush and pen are being sent to our boys in the trenches, and each breathes a message redolent of home as no more serious mementoes could. [2]

When the Gumnut Corps marched off to war they marched into the hearts of a nation and they have continued their invasion ever since. Their contribution to the Australian pictorial propaganda of the First World War was pervasive and amusing and remains perhaps the only such work to survive with a timeless appeal. Obviously most of these ephemeral productions were conceived for an adult audience, although any age group could and did appreciate them. Gibbs felt that her sudden elevation to national acclaim was unlikely to be sustained once the war finished. No doubt she was as surprised and as pleased as the publisher when her five booklets kept reprinting after 1918 in order to satisfy widespread public demand.

These booklets consisted of a text with 11 sepia illustrations, a colour frontispiece and a colour illustration pasted on to the front cover. While the format remains as a tribute to the design skills of May Gibbs, the limited use of colour was largely dictated by economic and technical restrictions within the Australian printing industry at the time. The year in which the first two booklets appeared (1916) was, coincidentally, the year that first saw significant colour printing in Australian books: *The Art of Frederick McCubbin* and Ida Rentoul Outhwaite's *Elves & Fairies* were both issued by the Melbourne firm of Lothians. Angus & Robertson's launching of the May Gibbs booklets was an equally imaginative publishing venture in Sydney, which quickly caught and sustained public interest.

In contrast to the sumptuous volume *Elves & Fairies,* Gibbs' booklets were cheap, diminutive and appealed to a mass market. She was establishing a robust and Australiana-based vision that contrasted strongly with the English style and sentiment of much of Ida Rentoul Outhwaite's work, which had dominated local children's books for the past decade. These contrasting approaches were to characterise Australian children's books for at least a generation and their effect is still evident.

Although today it may be difficult to fully comprehend the novelty of Gibbs' booklets and the public's reaction heightened by war, it is certain that their charm has been maintained. Each double-page spread is a compact unit; each page of text within its decorative border complements its full-page sepia illustration. Together the pages achieve the effect of a peepshow vision into a small world of wonders. The stage atmosphere with its pantomimic costumes and music hall head-dresses, its rambunctious happenings entirely located in the foreground and innocently enacted by tumbling putti or mock coy chanteuses (depending on one's point of view), is often so strong that the reader is free to ponder upon the character's real pedigree and assumed audience.

Within this context it is interesting to

Double-page spread from BORONIA BABIES by May Gibbs, Sydney, 1917.

'The Gum Blossom Ballet' by May Gibbs from SNUGGLEPOT AND CUDDLEPIE.

note that May Gibbs and Norman Lindsay were contemporaries and that the innocent world of naked gumnut babies was created at a time when Lindsay was first introducing his buxom, naked courtesans and bacchanalian revellers to an adult audience.

On the international scene, a valid comparison could be made with Beatrix Potter. May Gibbs cannot fail to have known and envied the phenomenal success of Potter's most productive years, 1901–1913, when the majority of her nursery classics were published. These were also the years that Gibbs was studying in London and both illustrators have many similar qualities in their work.

Potter's Peter Rabbit and his countryside setting is paralleled by Gibbs' gumnut babies and their bushland world. Initially both Beatrix Potter and May Gibbs favoured modest dimensions for the format of their books and showed a comparable regard for design that made each of their double-page spreads a compact unit. Both used a personal observation of nature to underpin any flights of fancy — their anthropomorphic creations are not just people in disguise; they display closely observed animal characteristics.

In their private lives, coincidentally, both women were also strongly alike. Both found it difficult to break away from a restrictive family circle and establish independent lifestyles and careers, both married late (Potter at 47 in 1913 and Gibbs at 42 in 1919) and both were happy to work in relative isolation. As authors, neither of them spare us the truth about the random perils of the natural world and out of the common objects of their miniature range they created a microcosm of the world. Most significantly, there is a shared feeling that the events described continue endlessly below the level of human observation.

'A Happy Family' by May Gibbs from LITTLE OBELIA*, Sydney, 1921.*

When May Gibbs spoke of her gumnut babies as being 'born', she emphasised the organic derivation of her folklore. Her bushland babies, and particularly the Banksia Men, have become so intimately associated with our vision of the Australian bush that it is difficult to divorce fact from fantasy. Anyone familiar with her illustrations cannot walk through the bush without 'seeing' some of her characters or at least evidence of their passing.

But the native flora which they embody does not make them into the traditional flower fairies so beloved of late Victorian and Edwardian childhood.Gibbs admitted, in fact, that 'ordinary,conventional fairies with wands and starry crowns never did appeal' [3]. Her creations have a certain imaginative rigour, a robust quality, which relates well to the perils of the Australian bush.

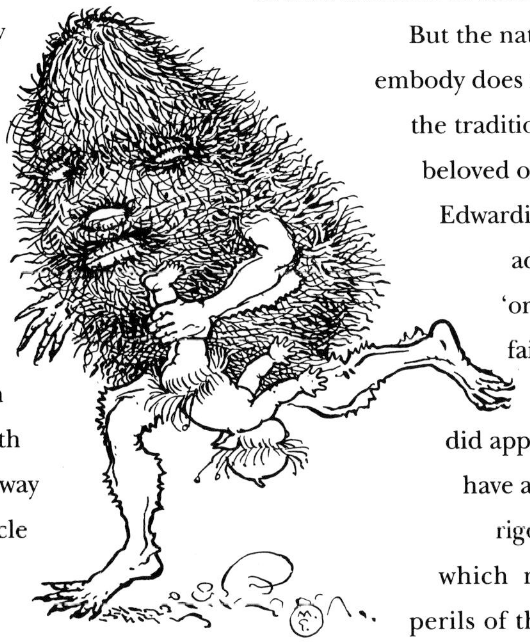

'The Wicked Banksia Man' by May Gibbs from SNUGGLEPOT AND CUDDLEPIE*; the first pictorial representation of these dreaded creatures.*

It is a world of fantasy anchored by quiet realism, even satire. Unlike other Australian children's book illustrators of the time, May Gibbs added a dimension of menace to this world — the Banksia Men. By adding this quality to her work she created a more rounded moral world in which her small dramas could be enacted.

In 1918 Gibbs issued her first proper Australian children's book, *Snugglepot and Cuddlepie: Their Adventures Wonderful* with its all important introductory message from the author: 'Humans. Please be kind to all Bush Creatures and don't pull flowers up by the roots'.

The human world that lurks beyond the horizon is always a presence in the world of the gumnut babies; there is the alarming possibility of actual human contact; the threat that humans will invade this Lilliputian world, marauding and mistreating the bush and its creatures. And increasingly the human world did encroach on Gibbs' fantasy setting as she created anthropomorphic characters that came to inhabit what she finally called 'Gumnut Town', a place whose comedy, satire and social comment was derived from Gibbs' own world.

One of a number of World War I postcards that carried a distinctive Australiana message to thousands of troops. Gibbs' matronly kookaburra figure was the first in a line of anthropomorphic characters that gave humour and vitality to her work.

A genealogy for the inhabitants of Gumnut Town is not difficult to find. Twenty years before *Snugglepot and Cuddlepie, Dot and the Kangaroo* came prefaced with a similar conservationist's plea:

To the children of Australia, in the hope of enlisting their sympathies for the many beautiful, amiable, and frolicsome creatures of their fair land; whose extinction, through ruthless destruction, is being surely accomplished.

The moral force of this attitude is conveyed most effectively through the kangaroo figure who rescues Dot, cares for her, but is almost shot when returning Dot to her home. The kangaroo becomes a mother figure for Dot, a maternal character that links the world of the bush with the human realm. Gibbs' use of the kookaburra in exactly the same way provided her with an even more effective anthropomorphic character.

The motherly kookaburra, which made its debut on a series of First World War postcards, was May Gibbs' first and most successful anthropomorphic creation. There was a dumpy maternity about these kookaburras who present a confident middle-class attitude in exhibiting and validating home values and domestic virtues. As part of the graphic propaganda of the war, May Gibbs produced two suites of six postcards almost all of which feature the kookaburra and family. One of the most effective proclaims, 'Your old Aunts are very anxious about you', and pictures two

The first and most significant poster ever issued by the Department of Public Health, Division of Maternal and Baby Welfare. May Gibbs combines a traditional figure from English folklore with the unique Australian character to produce a graphic icon.

One of the rarest collections of May Gibbs' comic strips (1920) with its appealing dustwrapper showing the peepshow vision of a miniature world beneath the gum trees.

matronly and bespectacled kookaburras knitting for the troops with cups of tea perched at their side. The kookaburra is also the first bush character to appear in anthropomorphic guise in the gumnut booklets. Here she appears again in adult human pose, amused by the gumnut babies and slightly cynical.

This role is then extended in Gibbs' writing where the kookaburra takes on the attributes of a wise teacher overseeing the gumnut babies' safety and education. In May Gibbs' first major children's book, *Snugglepot & Cuddlepie* (1918), the kookaburra is the first anthropomorphic character introduced and it is specifically in order to offer a warning:

These Humans ... are as bad as bad, but there must be bad things in this world as well as good. It would be very awkward for me if there were no snakes to eat.

This Gumnut Town philosophy is also presented in a full-page illustration where the wise kookaburra is seen to be the Australian equivalent of the owl in English folklore.

This effective linking of folklore is, however, seen to very best effect in Gibbs' use of the kookaburra in her poster for Baby Health Clinics of 1920. This poster coupled a character from European folklore, the stork, with a unique Australian identity, the kookaburra, and so brought together a double-edged piece of nostalgia and appeal. There are no intrusive human characters and yet the propagandist intent of the work is clearly directed beyond Gumnut Town to the human world. In May Gibbs' words: 'I hardly like delivering the Goods Mrs Kookaburra them Humans is so Gum careless of 'em.'

Perhaps the most important element in Gibbs' conception was its Australiana idiom. Nothing so effectively nationalistic had been seen in Australian poster art before. It went on to grace the cover of something like a million copies of the Department of Health's handbook for mothers, which remained current from 1931 to 1959 in 33 editions! As a piece of graphic propaganda her design was a perfect combination of characters, sentiment and appeal.

The projected audience would not have wanted or perhaps even appreciated graphic experimentation: here was an alphabet of art they could immediately read. By 1920 Gibbs' pictorial vocabulary of the motherly kookaburra and the endearing gumnut babies was firmly established in Australian nurseries as an indispensable part of the Australian child's upbringing and imaginative territory.

May Gibbs' image became synonymous with baby care in a programme that sought to educate the Australian mother and reduce the alarming infant mortality rate of the day. The maternal figure of the kookaburra and its parallel in the Australian nursery became the domestic exemplar of the proud national concept of the 'Motherland'. The war front was relocated into the nurseries of Australia, only now the enemy was disease, lack of baby care facilities and ignorance. The weapon was a campaign to educate mothers into a role as nation builders.[4]

The initial use of the kookaburra figure and its long-term appeal clearly indicate the power of folklore upon national sentiment. The poster did not show a careless or neglectful mother, an accusing nurse or a suffering baby. Instead of alienating an audience by negative images, the poster invited them to make the connection between fantasy and reality. Even the text itself is couched in scribbly gum writing rather than more official and perhaps threatening typography.

The serious message is imparted as a humorous meeting between two birds whose anthropomorphic stance invites us to see a harmony between the human world and the natural world, the Australian home and the Motherland, and the human realm and Gumnut Town.

Gumnut Town was eventually 'peopled' by a whole community of bush creatures. As well as the kookaburra, the main anthropomorphic characters were the kangaroo, the lizard, the bandicoot and the koala. But always encroaching on the Town's perimeter and a lurking presence in the background were the Banksia Men.

They are usually described as Big Bad Banksia Men and so share their alliterative name with the Big Bad City, the human realm and counterpart of Gumnut Town. The Banksia Men, however, have none of the social organisation or sense of community displayed by their small victims. They are more of an archaic, elemental force, which balances the moral equation in the world of the gumnuts.

By adding knobbly legs and muscular,

May Gibbs' imagery was popularised on all fronts including this 1920s piece of sheet music.

THE LONE HAND
May Gibbs
6D.
JANUARY
1914
egistered at the G.P.O., Sydney, for transmission by
post as a Newspaper.

grasping arms to the Banksia Men and giving them the language of yokels, May Gibbs created a creature that has haunted the nurseries of generations of Australian children. Just what we are to make of their origin is uncertain since no explanation is ever given. Like the gumnut babies and their flower counterparts, they simply *are* and we must accept that their conflict has always been a part of bush lore. Even so, it is interesting to speculate on the Banksia Men's wartime origin, their consuming and irrational hatred and their hairy appearance, which contrasts so distressingly with the infant nakedness and vulnerability of the gumnut babies!

Gumnut Town was established as a miniature world of ceaseless activity in the Australian bush where small dramas, comic events and fantastic adventures unfold beneath the eyes of humans, yet remain undiscovered. It is an extraordinary interplay of botanical fact and bushland fantasy or, on another level, a vision of everyday life in anthropomorphic guise. Yet however it is evaluated, May Gibbs' landscape of the imagination is never far removed from reality; her whole vision is anchored by as close a personal observation of bush life and creatures as of human follies and foibles.

Gumnut Town was not a microcosm that sprang fully formed from May Gibbs' imagination. It evolved as new characters were introduced, new imaginative territory annexed and relationships between the characters developed. In its initial stages Gumnut Town is simply called a 'village' and features a hatshop, a cabstand, a refreshment stall, a band, a theatre, the Gum Inn and the Cob Webb & Co. clothes shop. Domestic interiors and accessories are partly delineated but this is hardly a townscape as yet. It is not until the end of May Gibbs' first trilogy of books (1918–21) that Snugglepot and Cuddlepie reach the safely of what is termed Gumnut Town. It is there that Snugglepot builds a house and settles into an evolving social order.

The third volume, *Little Obelia*, was published in 1921 and only four years later Gibbs began the first of her comic strips, which were to run for more than 40 years! It is in these strips, over 2,000 of them, that the concept of Gumnut Town is fully developed and explored. Significantly, the very last frame of the very last comic strip Gibbs drew (published 10 September 1967) centred on her kookaburra figure — it was an association that had lasted over 50 years!

It is in these comic strips and Gibbs' later books that Gumnut Town undergoes its final metamorphosis. Indeed, there is a sense in which it seems to grow organically as the books unfold. Initially it was a town set high above prying human eyes:

Textual illustration by May Gibbs from LITTLE OBELIA, *Sydney, 1921. Mr Lizard and Snugglepot settle back in rough-hewn bush furniture, a feature of the interiors of Gumnut Town.*

'The road to Big Bad City' by May Gibbs from LITTLE OBELIA.

'The hurry-go-round' by May Gibbs from NUTTYBUB AND NITTERSING.

In the Big Gumtrees live the little Gumnut Babies. If you could climb to the very tiptop branches there you would find their little round houses, with the little round windows, and little round doors; hanging in the shelter of the leaves, warmed by the Sun, cooled by the Breezes, and kept clean and bright by the Rain. Up and down the branches where the spots of Sunlight chase the shadows — go the busy little Gumnut people. They are almost impossible to see because their little pink bodies look like the sunspots on the bark, and their bright green caps look like the leaves, and their big blue eyes are just the colour of the sky ... Yes, they are very hard to see, but there they are. Building their houses, making their bread, and minding their children in the daytime, and climbing into their beds and going to sleep at night. Just like Humans.

But their bread is made of grass roots, and their beds are leaves, swung up like hammocks, and their children don't wear any clothes.[5]

This aerial perspective changes in the mid–1920s as Gumnut Town becomes even more of a microcosm of the larger human world and a vehicle for social comment, comedy and satire. Even so, it should not be imagined that Gumnut Town became a topographically precise location in May Gibbs' mind, writing or illustrations. Beatrix Potter produced an environment for Peter Rabbit in sufficient detail to be able to visualise the complete layout of a village, but May Gibbs left her imaginative townscape as a more organic concept. This concept depicted characters, their accessories and furnishings and their immediate settings. In her later comic strips this becomes more of an earthbound scene with dumpy little English-looking cottages combined with an Australian setting of bush huts and bush furniture.

What May Gibbs drew on for her rough-hewn shelters and their household effects was an Australian pioneering tradition of using whatever was at hand and making do with makeshift and recycled materials. Such a tradition was to receive new impetus in the years immediately after May Gibbs' comic strips first started, as the Depression forced people to return to an earlier and more frugal way of life.

There is bush furniture, such as a chair of gnarled branches for the kookaburra and diminutive stools for the gumnuts, simple log benches, stick chairs and log cradles. There are also less funtional pieces, which are really bush toys. Thus we find gumnut cars, beetle carts and sledges, scooters and the most imaginative bush toy of all, the hurry-go-round from *Nuttybub and Nittersing.* All these help make much of Gumnut Town akin to a playground in miniature.

This play element becomes one of the overriding features of the comic strips, and the butt of the many mischievous pranks by Bib and Bub is usually Mr and Mrs Koala. These two figures provide an image of total domesticity in the village life and setting that Gumnut Town achieved. They are like foster parents to the gumnut babies and much more a part of the everyday world than Mrs Kookaburra ever was.

Although Gumnut Town is not a streetscape found in any directory it is part of the imaginative landscape of young Australians. May Gibbs created white Australia's first popular visual mythology.

'The Cabstand', by May Gibbs from SNUGGLEPOT AND CUDDLEPIE.

'The Boat Race' by May Gibbs from NUTTYBUB AND NITTERSING*, 1923.*

We can empathise with Gibbs' characters and dramas because we can recognise elements of our world in her so-called fantasy. In one of her most successful illustrations, 'The Boat Race' (1923), we share in the feelings of daring and trepidation that animate these small sailors. Their body language and vulnerable appeal do not isolate them in a fantasy world beyond human recognition.

The illustration also encapsulates the strength and characteristics that mark May Gibbs' illustrations as major contributions to the fantasy genre. 'The Boat Race' is a sepia and ink work and an imaginative and illustrative masterpiece. Without the advantage of colour, Gibbs created an illustration all the more striking and effective for its austerity. The pattern and play of the water are conveyed economically and provide a foil to the smooth curve of the billowing sail as the leading gumnut boat bursts out of the page carrying its wide-eyed crew who seem somewhat alarmed at their own daring. The drama and appeal in their small faces is a tribute to the trained miniature artist in May Gibbs. Nothing distracts from this foreground drama: the perspective of the gumnut fleet is conveyed in less precise lines.

By the 1920s May Gibbs was a household name throughout Australia. Her on-going children's books and comic strips, all of which featured the gumnut babies, maintained their post-war popularity along with gumnut fabric, badges, textbook illustrations, handkerchiefs, calendars, additional bookmarks and other ephemera. (The only other character in Australian children's literature to achieve comparable coverage to the gumnut babies was Ginger Meggs.) In 1920 *Little Ragged Blossom* appeared, followed by *Little Obelia* (1921), *Nuttybub and Nittersing* (1923) and *Chucklebud and Wunkydoo* (1924). All these titles were reprinted throughout the decade and at least seven collected Bib and Bub comic strips were also published during this period. Gibbs' comic strips, in fact, were published throughout Australia and New Zealand between 1924 and 1967! Most of her efforts from the 1930s onwards went into these strips and while they kept her in work, their deadly repetition and the constant need to meet a deadline must ultimately have become a burden.

By the mid-1930s very few reprints or new works were appearing and the Depression disrupted attempts to reach an international audience. Furthermore, the Second World War was not the imaginative catalyst to Gibbs' work which its predecessor had been and its effect on local publishing was ruinous. A second generation of fantasy illustrators entered into competition with Gibbs and their inferior work was presented in cheap formats and flooded the market.

Like Ida Rentoul Outhwaite, May Gibbs found that after the war the audience for outstanding fantasy illustration was sadly fickle. Unsympathetic reprintings did little to introduce her work favourably to a new generation of young Australians and only three new titles appeared: *Scotty in Gumnut Land* (1941), *Mr & Mrs Bear and Friends* (1943) and *Prince Dandelion* (1953). The characters in these titles occupy more of a domestic environment than before and together with an apparent lack of imaginative spontaneity, they can hardly be singled out as Gibbs' best work.

May Gibbs married James Kelly in 1919 when she was forty-two. The marriage was childless and she appeared to have little domestic or social inspiration for her work. It seems that she grew increasingly shy, retiring, and agoraphobic, and that she did not even enjoy contact with fellow artists. It was an acknowledged fact that Gibbs came to rely on the few outsiders who were permitted to broach her domain for incidents to include in her long-running comic strips. Her last housekeeper has recounted how Gibbs eagerly awaited her return after the weekend in order to learn of family incidents and comic situations, which May Gibbs then incorporated into her work.

In 1955 official recognition came in the form of an MBE although sadly, May Gibbs was already slipping in to the life of a recluse. When she died on 27 November 1969, the copyright on all her works passed to the New South Wales Society for Crippled Children and the Spastic Centre of New South Wales. At the time her passing made front page news. Many Australians thought May Gibbs had died years before and the shock they experienced on learning that she had, in fact, survived in their midst for so long brought a poignant reminder of their childhood.

Finally, it is May Gibbs' early work, pre–1925, which still remains her most appealing. It was not imitative of any other illustrator and for all its fantasy and charm, it never became merely cute. There is always some small detail to be found in a May Gibbs' drawing that repays close scrutiny and brings us back again and again to her miniature dramas.

Endnotes

1 *Sydney Morning Herald*, 'Women's Section,' 12 November 1953, p.4.

2 *Sunday Sun*, 11 March 1917, p.14.

3 *Women's World*, 1 December 1922, p.13.

4 'First Australian Baby Week', *Lone Hand*, 2 March 1920, p.13.

5. May Gibbs, *Nuttybub and Nittersing*, Osboldstone & Co., Melbourne, 1923, pp.1–2.

'The Water-Race' by Ruby Winckler from WHO'S WHO IN THE LAND OF NOD, *Boston, 1915.*

Forgotten Sydney Illustrators

Ruby Winckler, Olive Crane, Barbara Macdonald, Margaret Clark

If Melbourne has its forgotten fantasy illustrators so too does Sydney, although they do not form as coherent a clique as their southern counterparts. While some Sydney illustrators took elements of Melbourne's 'Elves and Fairies' school, others adopted a robust Australiana vision.

Many of these Sydney illustrators undertook more of a commercial art training than the academic art training offered by the National Gallery School of Painting in Melbourne. Sydney was certainly a mecca for aspiring commercial artists and illustrators early in the twentieth century. May Gibbs and Dorothy Wall, who arrived prior to the First World War, were not alone in seeing more opportunities in their line in Sydney than in Melbourne.

There were at least two major reasons why this geographical preference was established and maintained. In the first place the major local art school, the Julian Ashton School (which was founded in 1896), placed less of an emphasis on 'high art' by favouring graphic work, printmaking and commercial possibilities. Secondly, there were established business interests in Sydney that provided a commercial outlet for the talent that originated from Julian Ashton's or was attracted to Sydney, such as publishers William Brooks, Angus & Robertson and the New South Wales Bookstall Company; printers and stationers such as John Sands and H. C. Swain; the *Lone Hand* and *Smith's Weekly*, and pioneering commercial art studios such as Smith & Julius.

'Simple Simon' by Ruby Winckler from WHO'S WHO IN THE LAND OF NOD.

In chronological terms, the first 'forgotten' illustrator is Ruby Winckler (1886–1974), who studied at the Julian Ashton School early in the twentieth century and became a friend of the Lindsay family. She makes a brief appearance in Rose Lindsay's memoirs: 'I particularly remember ... Ruby Winckler ... [who] used to laugh uproariously'. [1]

The impact of the Lindsay family style as black and white artists is clearly evident in much of Ruby Winckler's work. Many of her early pen and ink drawings, as reproduced in the *Lone Hand*, for example, are virtually indistinguishable from those of her namesake Ruby Lindsay. Winckler's later and unpublished illustrations to *The Odyssey* [2] rival Norman Lindsay's own work for *The Satyricon* in their graphic satire, energy and pen control.

Today, however, Ruby Winckler's work is totally forgotten. A revival of interest is overdue if only for the fact that Ruby achieved the rare distinction of having two of the children's books she illustrated, *Arabian Night's Entertainment* and *Who's Who in the Land of Nod* published in America as early as 1915. This makes her the first Australian-born illustrator of children's books to reach an international audience. Ida Rentoul Outhwaite only achieved the same profile in England in 1921 and in America in 1929. After this achievement, Ruby Winckler returned to Australia.

Ruby Winckler contributed sporadically to Society of Artists exhibitions in Sydney between 1907 and 1918 and to Society of Women Painters exhibitions between 1913 and 1918. Even with this slight exhibition profile she was singled out for praise on more than one occasion:

I remember her best by her magnificent frieze ... [exhibited in the Society of Artists' Spring exhibition October 1908]. It caught the eye, I remember of Mr. Ernest Wunderlich, and he secured it. [3]

Ruby Winckler was doubtless inspired by the burgeoning Australian school of black and white illustration at the time and may even have been schooled on the popular series of Readers illustrated by D. H. Souter. Certainly his pen work provides another ready comparison with her own mature style. Both of Winckler's American publications are distinguished by the control and elegance of her pen work as well as by a strong regard for intricate patterning. With these characteristics, and her effective use of white space, Ruby aligns herself with Souter's stylish vision.

Ruby Winckler was perhaps the first woman who trained at the Julian Ashton School to pursue a career as a children's book illustrator. In this respect she was the immediate forerunner of Olive Crane (1895–1935) [4], who joined the School after graduating from Sydney University in 1917. Already Crane was known locally for the illustrative emphasis in her work and a keen desire to develop its commercial possibilities.

Because of Ruby Winckler's lamentably small artistic output, Olive Crane became the most significant female illustrator to emerge from the Julian Ashton School. By 1919 she began to exhibit with the Society of Artists and showed with them as a minor,

'Bo Peep saw the Queen' by Olive Crane from THE CITY OF RIDDLE-ME-REE*, Sydney, 1918.*

'Sing a Song a Sixpence' by Barbara Macdonald from A NEW BOOK OF OLD RHYMES, *Sydney, 1920.*

though regular, contributor until 1930. Her broader public debut was achieved in the publication of *The City of Riddle-Me-Ree*, a children's booklet of verses by Zora Cross. Thereafter Olive Crane's talent was in demand and two further volumes of poetry *The Betty Songs* and *The Sleeping Sea Nymph* followed in 1920 and 1921.

Crane's exhibition profile as well as her publishing profile was consolidating and critical opinion promised her 'a prominent future'. [5] However, Crane realised that her career in the small art world of children's book illustration could not be extended further on the local scene. She consequently travelled abroad to London and Paris where she lived between 1922 and 1926.

During these years she furthered her studies, undertook commissions for book illustrations and dust wrapper designs (primarily of adult titles), developed the commercial art side of her talent and learned to etch. Her most significant children's book illustrations during this period were for three E.V. Lucas works published in the early 1920s: *The Flamp, The Ameliorator* and *The Schoolboy's Apprentice*. Illustrations from the first two books were exhibited in the (Sydney) Society of Artist's Annual Exhibition for 1926. Crane maintained her exhibition profile in Sydney throughout the 1920s by sending such works home for exhibition. This kept her name before the Australian public.

Crane returned to Sydney in 1926 to marry the noted watercolourist, Kenneth MacQueen. Her subsequent isolation in a small farming community in northern New South Wales effectively halted her artistic career. Her tragically early death in 1935 robbed a young family of a wife and a mother and Australia of a talented artist. Thereafter, the career of her husband overshadowed any posthumous profile Olive Crane may have achieved. [6]

Mainstream children's publishing in Sydney began in 1916 with the modestly presented gumnut booklets of May Gibbs.

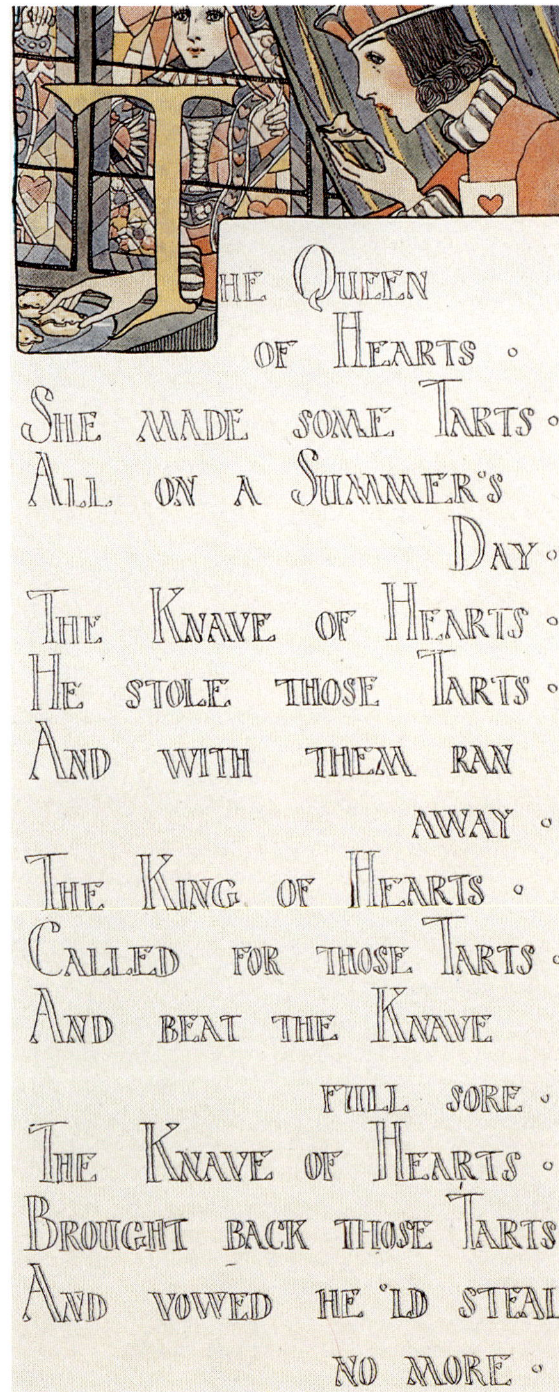

'The Queen of Hearts' by Barbara Macdonald from A NEW BOOK OF OLD RHYMES.
This conjunction of the art press with children's publishing produced the most elegant children's book in Australian history.

Coincidentally, another ambitious publishing venture began at the same time in Sydney and had some input into children's book production.

The art press in Australia as an on-going activity was most certainly a Sydney phenomenon and had been centred in that city since late 1916 when the publishing company 'Art in Australia' and the periodical of the same name were both launched. Before this the technical challenge of colour printing as well as the aesthetics of book design, typography and layout were largely ignored, if considered at all. The buying public necessary to sustain a company like 'Art in Australia' and appreciate its standards was never substantial in these pioneering years. How much rarer then was it to find children's books produced in Australia at this time with an equal regard for printing excellence and stylish production? The answer is that only a handful of stylish children's publications appeared and many of these were probably subsidised in some way by the author or illustrator to offset the financial risk. Two of the most lavish Australian children's books of the day only appeared because of such outside assistance. *Elves & Fairies* (1916) was promoted with entrepreneurial zeal by Outhwaite's husband, who guaranteed a certain number of sales; *The White Butterfly* (1921) was underwritten by its author Ethel Jackson Morris, according to correspondence between her and the printer. Another example of this 'subsidised publishing' was the first children's book published by 'Art in Australia' — Barbara Macdonald's *A New Book of Old Rhymes* (1920).

Even more than *Elves & Fairies*, this work has many of the attributes of a de luxe art book. The text is calligraphic and entirely subsidiary to the illustrations. Each laid-out block of rhyme is also a design element in itself, which balances its accompanying illustration. Although the book is not described as a limited edition, it is obvious that at one guinea each, perhaps less than 100 were actually printed. The unusual format of the book also entitles it to consideration as a work of art: each of the 13 illustrated (unbound) sheets is printed only on one side and encased in a portfolio tied with ribbons. An advertisement for subscribers stressed 'that the whole series can be framed if desired'. [7] As a precious object this lavish production could hardly have been produced in Australia at this time as a straightforward commercial entity. Captain W. Ian Macdonald, the illustrator's husband, was a nephew of Sir Rupert Clarke and it was he who underwrote the publishing costs. [8]

Whether an audience of children ever actually beheld the work is doubtful. What is certain, however, is that *A New Book of Old Rhymes* is an almost unparalleled achievement in the Australian publishing field: an item of children's literature produced to exacting art press standards.

Two years later, Barbara Macdonald illustrated *Princess Herminie and the Tapestry Prince*, the second and final children's book to be published by 'Art in Australia'. This time the format was much less precious and Princess Herminie is actually presented in the house style of the magazine, *Art in Australia*. It shares the same shape, almost

'Jehaz and Abdon' by Barbara Macdonald from PRINCESS HERMINIE AND THE TAPESTRY PRINCE, *Sydney 1922.*
This illustrator's mastery of pen and ink place her in a line of artistic descent from D. H. Souter and Ruby Winckler.

'Mary, Mary, quite contrary' by Barbara Macdonald from A NEW BOOK OF OLD RHYMES.

the same size and has similar wrappers over card covers. The work's greatest strength, unlike its predecessor, does not lie in its colour work but in its meticulous pen and ink work. With this second minor masterpiece, Barbara Macdonald faded from the Sydney scene and probably returned to her English home.

The final member of this quartet of Sydney fantasy illustrators is the little-known Margaret Clark. She was born in Plattsburg near Newcastle, New South Wales, in 1901, although she grew up in Sydney. While still in her teens she was commissioned to produce illustrations for the confectionery manufacturers 'Sweetacres'. A small pamphlet, *Fairies,* was issued in 1918 to publicise a deluxe range of packaging, which consisted of small original watercolours mounted on to the lids of boxes of sweets. These delicate works were complimented for their 'versatility of fancy and capacity for infinite detail and imagery'. [9]

In 1920 Angus & Robertson suggested that she might attempt a more ambitious project and illustrate a book, but nothing eventuated. She attended the Julian Ashton School for one term and in November 1923, what was perhaps her first published illustration, appeared in the children's magazine, *Young Australia.* Thereafter, very short stories or poems with fantasy illustrations appeared in this and similar magazines. She contributed to the first issue of *Steele Rudd's Magazine* in July 1929 and in 1930 two large colour friezes (her last published works) were included as special supplements in the magazine, *Australian Childhood.*

In 1924 she exhibited with the Society of Women Painters and the high point of this exposure was her own solo exhibition two years later. In August 1926 she exhibited 23 fantasy watercolours at the Sydney Art Salon and was an unqualified success. The exhibition was a sell-out and it is both surprising and regrettable that an enterprising publisher did not promote this popular success still further. Only the month before Ida Rentoul Outhwaite had held her third Sydney exhibition and the obvious affinities between the two artists were pointed out by at least one critic:

[Margaret Clark's] work consists of pen drawings in colour of fairy subjects, such as have been made popular by Mrs. Ida Outhwaite, but these are by no means copies of the work of others; they are entirely original, and show in many cases much better drawing and imagination than many other exhibitors in this branch of art. [10]

Sadly, Margaret Clark's developing profile was not maintained. She married in 1929 and the illustrative output that was only beginning to reveal its full potential came to an end. The work of this self-effacing and unambitious artist was only brought to public attention again in 1986. [11]

Margaret Clark has acknowledged that she eagerly visited Ida Rentoul Outwaite's Sydney exhibitions and that she treasured this illustrator's books. She also remembers fondly a meeting with another children's book illustrator in Sydney, Harold Gaze. It

'The Florist Shop' by Margaret Clark.

'The Spirit of Mischief' by Margaret Clark.

Simple Simon
met a Pieman.
Going to the Fair.
Said Simple Simon
to the Pieman:
Let me taste
your Ware:
Said the Pieman
to Simple Simon:
Give me first
your Penny:
Said Simple Simon
to the Pieman:
Sir. I have not any:

'Simple Simon' by Barbara Macdonald from A NEW BOOK OF OLD RHYMES.

is in comparison with the work of these and similar fantasy illustrators that Margaret Clark's own work takes a worthy place. Her illustrations, which are really coloured pen and ink drawings, rely for their effect on dramatic silhouette: a full moon rising behind a steep hill or glimpsed through the trees. This is complemented with fine ornamentation and filigree touches of detail heightened with watercolour. Each illustration is a dramatic incident in itself, a static composition that conveys a story of immediate charm and appeal.

Although there is a lack of any unifying fantasy vision among this Sydney quartet, there is an undeniable individuality of talent. The career of each illustrator, however, seemed to occupy a distressingly short time span: Ruby Winckler's only known books were issued in 1916; Olive Crane's children's books between 1919 and 1926; Barbara Macdonald's between 1920 and 1922 and Margaret Clark's magazine contributions between 1923 and 1930.

In this decade and a half, the careers of Ida Rentoul Outhwaite and May Gibbs were at their greatest and have dominated our perception and evaluation to the exclusion of many minor figures. It is time that Australia's historical artscape was repopulated with these other figures, who not only throw the achievement of Outhwaite and Gibbs into greater relief, but also establish a more vital and varied illustrative milieu in Australia at the time.

ENDNOTES

1 Rose Lindsay, *Model Wife* Sydney: Ure Smith, 1967, pp. 8–9.

2 Ruby Winckler's illustrations to 'The Odyssey' were exhibited in the Society of Women Painters Annual exhibition, March 1917 and in the Society of Artists' Annual exhibition, December 1917.

3 'Australian Art & Artists,' *Building*, August 1915, p.128. See also 'The Sydney Pictures,' *Herald*, 5 November 1907, p.2.

4 Olive Crane was born 9 May 1895 and not 1896 as is usually quoted.

5 *Sydney Mail*, 19 January 1921, See also *Sydney Mail*, 14 September 1921.

6 The first retrospective exhibition of her work was not held until 1987 — at the New England Regional Art Gallery.

7 Advertisement in *The Home*, 1 December 1920, p.41.

8 Michael Richards, *People,Print & Paper* Canberra: National Library of Australia, 1988, p.59.

9 *Fairies: Being Original Drawings by Margaret Clark*, Sydney: [Sweetacres?] c.1918.

10 J. McNally, 'Fairy Drawings: Miss Margaret Clark's Work,' *Daily Telegraph*, 18 August 1926, p.11.

11 Retrospective exhibition curated by the author in the James Hardie Gallery, Sydney.

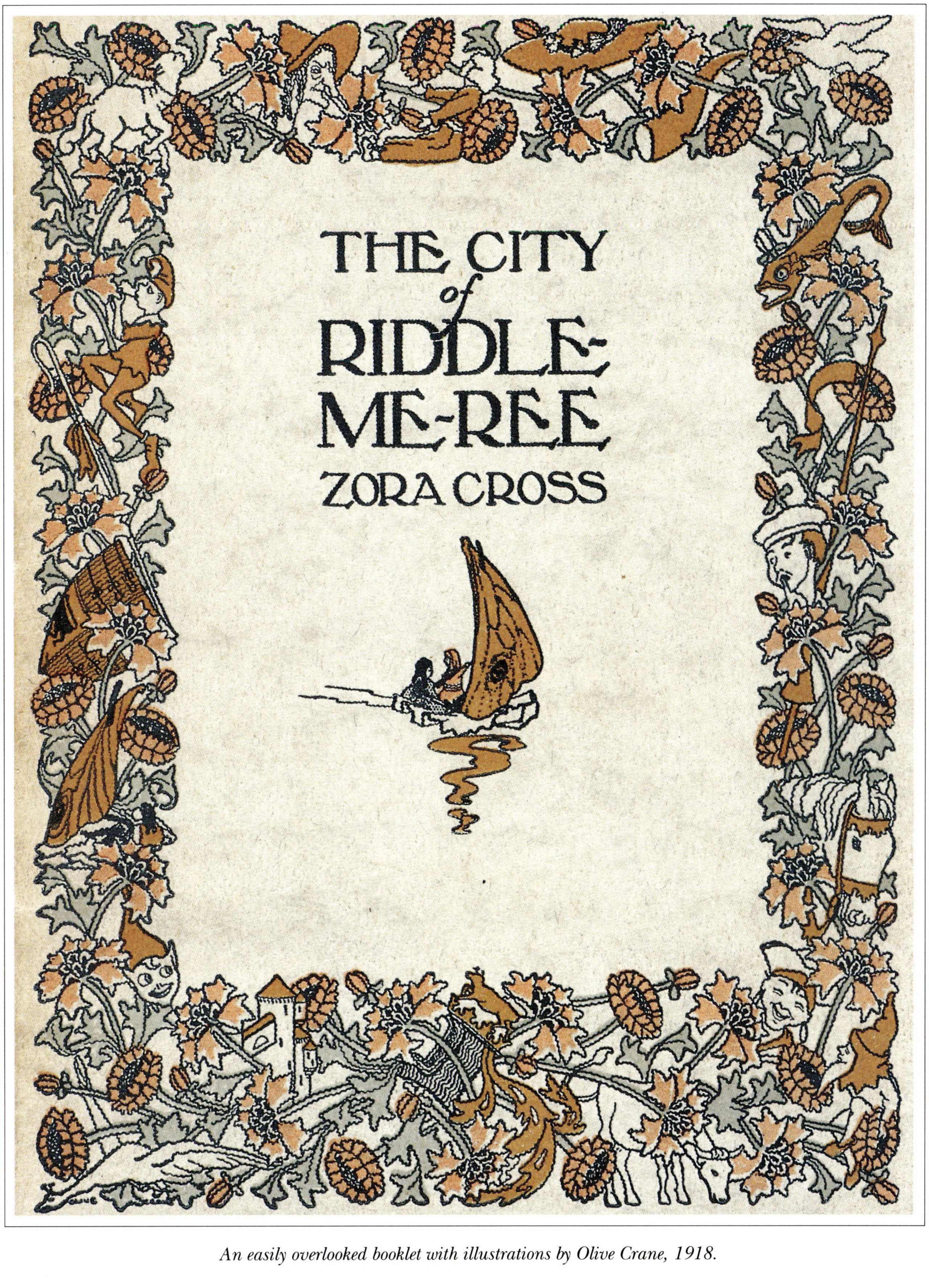

An easily overlooked booklet with illustrations by Olive Crane, 1918.

The Magic Pudding

Being the Adventures of Bunyip Bluegum.

The Lindsay Family

Norman, Lionel, Percy and Ruby

Until perhaps the 1970s, the only Australian children's book to command on-going attention from both a local and an international audience was Norman Lindsay's *The Magic Pudding*, first published in 1918 with illustrations by its author. In its own day it was virtually without parallel; today its appeal seems timeless and its classic status unchallenged. Although it is true that there were Australian forerunners such as *Bubbles* (1899) and *Gum Leaves* (1900), these were much less a coherent amalgam of text and illustration. They were really decorated books for children in which the pen and ink work embellished the text rather than extended its imaginative realm. Other works, such as *The Spirit of the Bushfire* (1989) with illustrations by G.W. Lambert and *Dot and the Kangaroo* (1899) with illustrations by Frank Mahoney, were not matched with pictures that did justice to their classic textual status. Along with *The Magic Pudding* perhaps the only other Australiana-based vision (an exception which therefore excludes Ida Rentoul Outhwaite) to so succinctly and immediately enrich the heart of a nation in both words and images, was May Gibbs' gumnuts.

Norman Lindsay (1879–1969) was a contemporary of May Gibbs (1877–1969) and his adult illustrations featuring naked revellers and bacchanalian orgies make an interesting contrast with the innocent escapades of May Gibbs' naked gumnuts. Some commentators have sought to find exotic interpretations in these parallels — what is more pertinent and revealing, however, is to look at the milieu the two shared as children's book authors and illustrators in wartime.

Gibbs' gumnut babies and their allies were as much a reaction against wartime despair and a contribution to Australia's pictorial propaganda as Norman Lindsay's magic pudding and boisterous koalas. The emerging war effort was unifying the country and there was a national and heartfelt sentiment that sought expression in patriotic symbols and images — in something robustly Australian.

This shared catalyst has previously been overlooked: Lindsay's inspiration for *The Magic Pudding* is usually seen as being his dissatisfaction with the traditional themes of children's literature:

For me there was only one flaw in the 'Alice' books and that was that Alice got nothing to eat in them ... Away back about the year 1915, I became involved in an argument about the best literary pabulum for young readers with a friend ... in his opinion, fairies, constituted its major theme for subject matter. I contested that ... if a kid was given a choice between fairies and food in typematter it would plump for food. [1]

The result was a story about a magic pudding which renewed itself after every slice was taken!

While this impetus is an acknowledged and much-quoted fact, it only accounts for the book's conception. The work's brash and assertive flavour, its Digger determination to flout authority and its high spirits are explained in more local and nationalistic terms:

... one very depressed night during the 1914 war, I was sitting glumly in my studio, and it was only as a desperate expedient to avert my thoughts from a war of mud and blood, that I picked up a notebook and started writing some nonsense about a bear named Bunyip Bluegum, and his Uncle Wattleberry's whiskers, and from then on the little book wrote itself. [2]

Bunyip Bluegum by Norman Linsday from THE MAGIC PUDDING, *Sydney, 1918.*

By this stage of his career the author/illustrator was a household name and it was reported that 'half a million Australians look for the work of Norman Lindsay every week'. [3] Colour printing was only in its infancy in Australia at the time and although all of Lindsay's illustrations in this first edition (apart from dust wrapper, cover and prospectus) were black and white, there is nothing mean or unappealing in the book's production. Indeed, Lindsay himself complained that at one guinea a copy, printed on art paper and with a prospectus it was being made into 'an art book ... quite beyond the reach of all young people'. [4]

Nevertheless the book has been consistently reprinted over the past 70 years and in 1968 a jubilee edition was published which included all the original black and white illustrations together with eight new colour plates. These additional plates were Lindsay's designs for the puppet show version first produced in Australia in 1958. As theatrical conceptions, these additional illustrations have comic strength and appeal.

At the time of *The Magic Pudding*'s publication, Angus and Robertson were also issuing *The Pen Drawings of Norman Lindsay.* Lindsay's name was more synonymous with adult cartoons and illustrations than work for a young audience. He had contributed minor illustrations to *A Health Reader* in 1908 and to a booklet of *Australian Nursery Rimes* in 1917, but these were not mainstream contributions to literature for young

Australians. His first novel, *A Curate in Bohemia*, had appeared in 1913 and was decidedly adult. Indeed, by this time Norman's fame, or notoriety, was seen as a national disgrace or a national asset, depending on one's allegiances.

After a sell-out exhibition in Sydney in 1909 his two major pictorial characters were firmly established in the public's eye: koalas and bare-breasted women. The common jibe credited Norman Lindsay with 'climbing to fame and fortune on koala's backs and women's tits'. [5] And certainly Lindsay's first pictorial love is clearly in evidence in *The Magic Pudding*: as his satirising talents were given free rein, the three koalas who career through the book reveal the comic inventiveness inherent in that unique Australian animal.

Norman Lindsay's illustrative style is radically different from that of other Australian illustrators working in a fantasy mode. Lindsay does not rely on decorative and ornamental effect; much of the time it is his use of white space that gives drama and action to his work. His characters frequently recede into this space thereby giving a strong sense of perspective, and the impression of a limitless horizon beckoning with adventures. Lindsay's illustrative line is pared down to its bare essentials, untrammelled by anything that would distract us from the strong narrative intent. By the time *The Magic Pudding* was published, Lindsay's style had been refined over 20 years of intense and dedicated effort. The result is a group of illustrations rendered with a bold, confident line that immediately established individual personality, poise

Dobson Dorking by Norman Lindsay from THE MAGIC PUDDING.

and character. There is perhaps no other illustrator, apart from Beatrix Potter, who managed to instil such personality and humour into their creations.

Contemporary reviews were rich in praise and quick to recommend this latest product from Lindsay's imagination:

One gets no shock of surprise at any new achievement of Norman Lindsay, for he has so accustomed his admirers to triumphs of self-expression in different forms of art that they live in an atmosphere of wonder as easily as changelings breathe the air of fairyland ... The story is interesting enough, and there are pearls of wisdom by the way that is trodden by Bill and Bunyip and Sam. Yet there is little in the letter-press that is not more directly and more humorously conveyed by the pictures. Can anybody else in the world depict the forms and faces of animals with such play of emotion? The last picture of all we lingered over with delight — the home in the tree was so alluring ... [6]

'Chunder Loo in Lookout' by Lionel Lindsay from the BULLETIN, *28 June 1917.*

'The tree house' by Norman Lindsay from THE MAGIC PUDDING .

The reviewer's final accolade and comment warrants further consideration. The last illustration is quite rightly singled out for praise and while not seeking to diminish its originality, it is instructive to place alongside it one of his brother Lionel's illustrations from the previous year. Lionel's 'Chunder Loo' illustrations were actually full-page advertisements in the *Bulletin* for Cobra Boot Polish and first appeared on 8 April 1909. Norman frequently stood in for his brother on these spirited drawings and the various characters, especially the dapper koala, delighted adults and children alike.

During the war years Lionel's drawings, understandably, were filled with Anzac lore and humour and the koala's exploits at the Front were another Lindsay family contribution to Australia's pictorial propaganda. In 1916 a selection of these exploits was published in book form: *The Adventures of Chunder Loo.* Although it was never acknowledged, this publication must surely have been another small catalyst towards the

'Chunder Loo bike riding' by Lionel Lindsay from THE ADVENTURES OF CHUNDER LOO*, Sydney, 1917.*

The Adventures of Chunder Loo
1/-
LIONEL LINDSAY

production of Norman's own children's book with tearaway koalas. These two tree-house illustrations certainly cause us to wonder as to the direction of artistic influence and inspiration.

Almost 20 years later Norman's only other book for children, *The Flyaway Highway* (Sydney: Angus & Robertson, 1936), was published. It has never enjoyed the acclaim of its forerunner and Norman himself described it as 'a job that went wrong ... not effective with either kids or grown-ups'. [7] The illustrations and the text lack the spontaneity, the comic invention and the rollicking exuberance of *The Magic Pudding.*

Perhaps the most interesting thing about its illustrations is revealed in a close look at the original pen and ink drawings. Almost all that feature the adolescent girl have her redrawn figure pasted over the original. In all cases it is an attempt to tone down the model's voluptuous curves and make her more suitable for a children's book. Apparently Norman found a lifetime's dedication to the depiction of well-endowed females difficult to circumscribe!

Lionel Lindsay (1874–1961) is not usually thought of as a children's book illustrator. He seems to have drifted into pictorial journalism, unlike Norman who steered a determined course in that direction. Once launched on his profession, however, Lionel embraced it and became the immediate catalyst for Norman's own debut into the same milieu.

Thereafter the two brothers worked side by side for a brief time, sometimes in tandem, so that their early work is almost indistinguishable. Lionel, however, was not content, or self-confident enough, to stay self-taught like Norman. He attended drawing classes at the National Gallery School (Melbourne), took lessons from the young George Coates and did figure drawing at the Victorian Artists' Society classes.

In the first decade of this century Lionel, like others in his family, found the new South Wales Bookstall Company a mainstay, even if its commissions were for hack illustrative work. Lionel's first work for a children's book would appear to be six colour illustrations for Amy Mack's *Bushland Stories* (Sydney: Angus & Robertson, 1910). Like his adult work for the Bookstall Company, these are undistinguished. The very small selection of 'Chunder Loo' drawings that were issued in book form in 1916 remain Lionel's most outstanding contribution to Australian children's book illustration. In the next decade he began to consolidate a career as critic and art historian and achieved international distinction for his rather formal wood-engravings. The pace and humour of his 'Chunder Loo' illustrations remind us of his more exuberant days and show another Lindsay making effective use of the koala image.

Although Lionel's profile generally, let alone as a children's book illustrator, was overshadowed by Norman, there were two other Lindsays who contributed to Australia's tradition of fantasy illustration who are even less remembered and acknowledged today: Percy Lindsay (1870–1952) and Ruby Lindsay (1885–1919).

Percy Lindsay was the eldest of the ten Lindsay children and was never as ambitious an artist as his energetic siblings.

'The March Past' by Percy Lindsay from THE MAGIC BILLABONG*, Sydney, 1928.*

He derived most of his sporadic income from illustrative work, particularly commercial art work, but in comparison with Norman, Lionel or Ruby his pen and ink line is tentative, his draughting uninspired and his figures awkward. Indeed, he seems to have resented spending time on illustrative work preferring instead to work on small landscape paintings in oils, which were his forte.

Percy illustrated only a small number of children's books. His two major commissions in this field were both fantasy titles: E.S. Emerson's *Santa Claus and a Sun-Dial* (Melbourne: George Robertson, 1909) and Thomas Grattan-Smith's *The Magic Billabong* (Sydney: Grattan Press, 1928). This last title is certainly Percy's best effort at children's book illustration and is a marine fantasy like May Gibbs' *Little Obelia* (1920) and Pixie O'Harris' *Pearl Pinkie and Sea Greenie* (1935). 'The March Past' from *The Magic Billabong* may be Percy's most effective illustration for a children's book, but his brusque cross-hatching and nervous line indicate a talent that was more comfortable in another medium.

In direct contrast, Ruby Lindsay was a hardworking, prolific and accomplished pen and ink artist. Because of her tragically early death in the influenza epidemic of 1919, Ruby Lindsay is one of the lesser known Lindsays. Nevertheless, the illustrations she left behind are sufficient proof of a talented artist cut short in her prime. Her early work has strong stylistic affinities with the work of Norman, who actually gave her an initial training in the handling of pen and ink. In her mature work, however, there is a gentleness and an ability to capture some of the magic of childhood, that sets her efforts apart as being uniquely her own.

Daryl Lindsay described his sister as 'never without a sketch-book in her hands'. [8] When Ruby moved to Melbourne in 1903 her three brothers, Norman, Lionel and Percy set an example to their young sister of mutual encouragement and industry. It would seem that no illustrative commission was too minor and no editor too parsimonious for the Lindsays to be frightened away from offering their work. Many short-lived publications from Brisbane (*Steele Rudd's Magazine*) to Adelaide (*The Gadfly*) were the training ground for all four. (Twenty years later in Sydney, a young Pixie O'Harris was to submit to a similar discipline to become perhaps the best woman pen and ink artist after Ruby Lindsay.)

It has been said that Ruby lacked the bravura and self-confidence of her brothers and their circle and this is certainly true. [9] Although she was hardly the technical equal of Norman, she was at least his counterpart in dedication and single-minded determination to become a black and white artist. Ruby does not appear to have had any formal art training and yet she was one of the very few Australian women artists establishing a career at the beginning of the twentieth century. By 1907, William Moore was using Ruby as an example to extol the possibilities of black and white work in his 'Careers for Australasian Girls' series. [10] The fact that the self-taught Ruby was able to take a role along with the first generation

'The Lamplighter came down the street' by *Ruby Lindsay from* NAUGHTY SOPHIA, *London, 1912.*

of professionally trained Australian women artists is a testimony to her dedicated application and industry.

In 1906 Ruby made her debut as another artist in the Lindsay family, extending their artistic hegemony in black and white illustration still further. Perhaps her first significant illustration appeared in *Steele Rudd's Magazine* in January 1906 and by August and September of that year she was contributing cover designs to that periodical. In February 1906 she first contributed to *The Gadfly* and by November Ruby's work began to appear in the *Lone Hand*. She steadily gained a reputation as another Lindsay who could be relied upon to produce competent black and white work for a wide range of purposes.

No doubt some of her initial popularity was due to her renowned, later legendary, beauty, a fact that may have made early opinions of her artistic worth rather subjective. Ruby's first book illustrations also began to appear in 1906: Steele Rudd's *Back at our Selection* included her work in company with that of other young illustrators. A. G. Stephens criticised the quality of illustration and Will Dyson, who later married Ruby, leapt to her defence with quick and gallant passion. Ruby's reputation, however, hardly seemed to suffer and Stephen's final words bear reconsideration:

> *... errors and shortcomings seem somehow to swing with the spirit of the whole performance, as if young Australia were flinging things around from sheer gladness of heart in a reckless and original manner of its own.* [11]

'Old Father Time' by Ruby Lindsay. Unidentified magazine illustration, c.1912.

'Gnomes' by Ruby Lindsay from NAUGHTY SOPHIA.

No finer summation of the bohemian fraternity in general and Ruby's own energy in particular could be found.

Until her marriage to Will Dyson in September 1909, Ruby's illustrations continued to appear regularly in Australian publications and she was an artist much in demand:

More refined in subject than the average work of Norman, Percy, or Lionel, and always with an excellent flavour of humour, those drawings of Ruby Lindsay that have so far appeared make the writer heartily cross because Ruby Lindsay does not draw more. [12]

In 1910, the year after Ruby's departure for London, an exhibition of more than 500 original illustrations from the *Bulletin* and the *Lone Hand* was held in Melbourne and Sydney and included three Ruby Lindsay works in company with others by Norman and Lionel Lindsay, George Lambert, Phil May, 'Hop' Will Dyson et al. By the time she left Australia for England, Ruby was a valued contributor to this fraternity of black and white artists.

Ruby continued to send work back to Australia to satisfy an obvious demand for her cartoons and began contributing to numerous English periodicals such as *London Opinion* and the *British Australasian.* Will Dyson's career as political cartoonist and caricaturist was forging ahead and Ruby seems, at last, to have had the opportunity to develop her own style without the inevitable comparisons being made between her work and that of the other Lindsays. Indeed, it was in an effort to establish an individual profile that she had begun to sign her work 'Ruby Lind'.

Ruby's daughter Betty was born in 1911 and thereafter Ruby quickly moved into book illustration on the English scene. Probably her first commission was for *Woman, Wedlock and the World* by 'Celt' (London: Gay & Hancock, 1911). This style of book, a combination of mild satire and humour, enabled Ruby to continue in the illustrative vein she had begun in Australia. At the time of her death in 1919, she was working on a series of such books by Sophie Loeb.

Ruby's most ambitious illustrative work was the children's fantasy *Naughty Sophia* by Winnifred Letts (London: Grant Richards, 1912) which contained a formidable total of 30 full-page black and white illustrations and more than 70 vignettes. It was a popular work and was issued the following year in an American edition and reissued in England as late as 1949. It showed a new side to Ruby's talent, one that confirmed the artistic development she was undergoing away from Australia.

In the Lindsay family ménage, Ruby still managed to be heard over the competing clamour of other, larger egos. In the competitive international world of book illustration, she continued to maintain a

career 'developing fresh graces of style and acquiring a new distinction of line'. [13] Her early death far from her homeland meant that knowledge and interest were not sustained in her work and the long productive lives of Norman and Lionel further deflected attention away from any possible posthumous profile.

Pen and ink illustration in Australia had scarcely gone through its first generation when these four Lindsays began their influential barrage. We can be grateful that some of their efforts were expended in the illustration of fantasy themes for Australian children's books.

ENDNOTES

1 Quoted in Hugh Anderson's *The Singing Roads*, Part I (Sydney: Wentworth Press, 1972), pp. 54–5.

2 Quoted in Harry Chaplin's *Norman Lindsay* (Sydney: Wentworth Press, 1969), p.12.

3 'Percy Lindsay, Artist', *Lone Hand*, June 1919, p.12.

4 Letter to George Robertson, October 1917, quoted in *Letters of Norman Lindsay* (Sydney: Angus & Robertson, October 1979), p.104.

5 John Hetherington, *Norman Lindsay: The Embattled Olympian* (Melbourne: O.U.P., 1973). p.68.

6 J.L.G.B. [John Le Gay Brereton], ['Review'], *Hermes*, v.24 (new series) no.3, November 1918, p.318.

7 Quoted in Harry Chaplin, op.cit., p.45.

8 Daryl Lindsay, *The Leafy Tree: My Family* (Melbourne: Cheshire, 1965), p.69.

9 Carol Mills, 'Ruby Lind: The little known Lindsay,' *This Australia*, v.3 no.3, Winter 1984, p.83.

10 William Moore, 'Careers for Australasian Girls IX — What the artist's life offers,' *New Idea*, v.6 no.13, December 1907, p.848.

11 A. G. Stephens, *Bulletin*, 18 October 1906, Red Page.

12 Grant Hervey, 'Black-and-white-Australia,' *Steele Rudd's Magazine*, v.3 no.9, October 1906, p.807.

13 'Ruby Lindsay,' *Herald* (Melbourne), 18 March 1919.

BLINKY BILL
JOINS THE ARMY
DOROTHY WALL
STORY and ILLUSTRATIONS
by DOROTHY WALL

Dorothy Wall

Creator of Blinky Bill

Just prior to the First World War, two remarkable women arrived in Sydney to pursue careers as graphic artists. Both had academic training on which to base their ambitions and both were breaking away from their families. Neither perhaps imagined that they would develop profiles as leading children's book illustrators and authors.

For May Gibbs, who arrived in 1913, the completion of her studies, her final hard won independence and the turmoil and heightened emotions of a world on the brink of war were all a giddy draught, even to a shy and sober 36 year-old. Dorothy Wall, almost 17 years younger than her fellow artist, arrived from New Zealand in 1914 with more modest ambitions. These were soon channelled into providing fashion drawings, advertising illustrations and layouts for the daily press, magazines and sales catalogues.

A ferment of artistic activity and diversity, of opportunities in an unprecedented range of illustrated magazines and in a flourishing commercial art scene brought Dorothy Wall to Sydney as surely as it did many others and provided her with her initial freelance opportunities. According to her own account, the very day she arrived in Sydney, she found work as an art-needlework designer and later, for several years, as a poster designer and commercial artist.[1] Certainly Dorothy Wall's family background, training, and brief work experience in New Zealand had prepared her for this versatility of career.

Dorothy Wall was born in New Zealand in 1894. Her father was an artisan and at one time taught plaster modelling and woodcarving at the Canterbury Technical School in Christchurch. In 1906 Dorothy entered the School of Art in Christchurch and the following year transferred to Wellington Technical

College, where her major artistic influence was provided by the teaching of Maud Sherwood. After completing her presumably rather limited art training, Dorothy Wall found work as a commercial artist and craft worker.

Most of her work throughout the next decade lies buried in an anonymous welter of commercial art, in ephemeral and presumably minor commissions. The only identified work that has come to light is a solitary example published in the *Lone Hand* of 1 October 1914, a noteworthy Australian debut for a new talent. This black and white fantasy drawing entitled 'The Cheat' depicts four grotesque and elongated figures playing cards. It appears to be quite a juvenile work, presumably from Wall's student days, although even so there is no reason why similar work should not have appeared thereafter in other magazines of the day. There was a flourishing market for black and white art; perhaps Wall was too busy establishing an independent lifestyle in Sydney and fulfilling more mundane commissions to follow up this initial success.

In this early illustration we can already identify compositional devices and pictorial choices that were to remain with Dorothy Wall throughout her life. For example, the device of straight, almost architectural, tree trunks silhouetted against a full moon, a predilection for patchwork detail in fabric and clothing, and a manner of depicting flowers as single stems dotting the countryside. But the most significant feature of this illustration is the grotesque figures. They became a standard feature of her work, appearing as late as 1939 in *Mickles & Muckles.*

It was not until 1920 that Dorothy Wall's first mature work appeared and moved her into direct competition with May Gibbs. During the war and for years afterwards, Gibbs produced handmade calendars, bookmarks and cards. Dorothy Wall developed a similar line after the war for the stationery firm of H. C. Swain and it was perhaps inevitable that she would next turn to writing and illustrating a children's book: *Tommy Bear and the Zookies* (1920).

By this time May Gibbs was a household name in Australia and Wall must have looked at Gibbs' phenomenal and sudden success with admiration as well as envy. Wall's reaction, however, took a practical turn and she wrote and illustrated her own first book, a modest production, really a booklet, of 16 pages with six colour plates.

In the past this book has only been noticed in a rather dismissive and cursory manner, but it deserves a more considered evaluation. Instead of reviving the grotesque fantasy figures that had appeared in the *Lone Hand*, Dorothy Wall was inspired to create a new character entirely, which was based on the koala. Although his friends the zookies, who lived in the treetops, are certainly kin to the gumnut babies, Tommy Bear is delightfully original and is the forerunner of Blinky Bill.

Unlike May Gibbs' stories, the antics of Tommy Bear are seen in an urban setting and there is more of the little boy than the koala in this anthropomorphic figure of

'The Cheats', Dorothy Wall's earliest known Australian illustration. Published in the Lone Hand, *1 October 1914.*

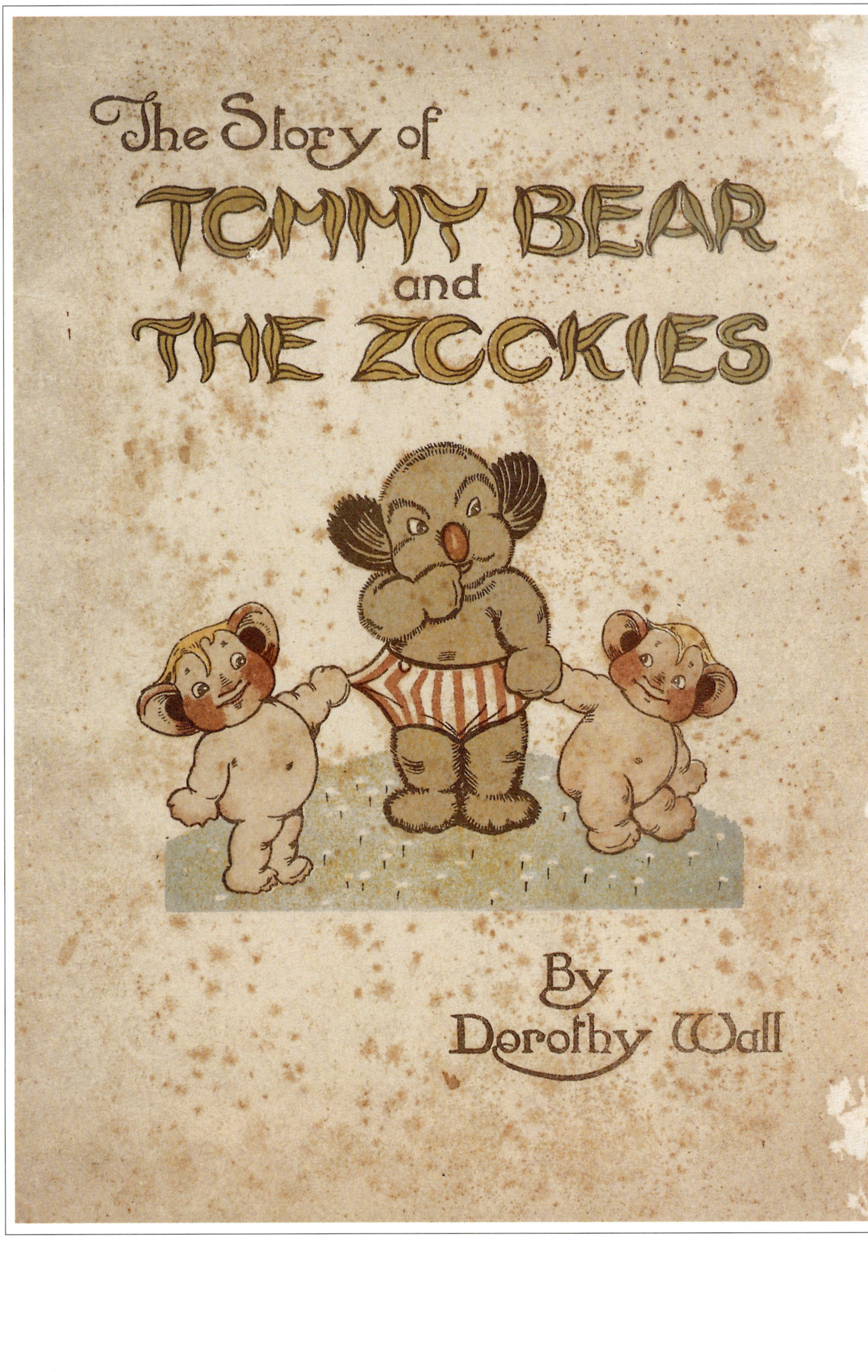
The Story of
TOMMY BEAR
and
THE ZOOKIES
By
Dorothy Wall

comedy. Nevertheless, the style and humour of this debut display a certain robust quality that contrasts favourably with what was sometimes a rather effete approach to fantasy writing and illustration by Wall's contemporaries. A romantic attachment that began at this time between Dorothy Wall and Andrew Badgery, a keen aviator, is acknowledged in the harum-scarum scene of Tommy Bear on the biplane. Overall, there is a charmingly naive and uncluttered quality to these illustrations, which was only matched in the much later booklet of similar size, *A Tiny Story of Blinky Bill* (c.1942).

Tommy Bear put Dorothy Wall's name before the public, albeit in a small way, and she was then commissioned to illustrate a volume of so-called Australian nature stories, *The Crystal Bowl* by J. J. Hall (1921). The initial interest she had shown in depicting Australian fauna was reaffirmed and extended here, somewhat influenced by May Gibbs' example. Gibbs' style, however, proved inimitable, and the book was an uneasy mixture of close bushland observation and an intrusive fantasy element.

What Dorothy Wall and other illustrators and authors failed to appreciate in their attempts to emulate May Gibbs' winning formula was that her gumnut babies and their companions were almost an organic derivation from the bush itself and not something forced into being merely for humorous and pictorial effect. This is not to say that *The Crystal Bowl* lacks appeal, but that the most successful illustrations are those which concentrate more on the realistic life of the bush. The work's other major limitation lies in the monochrome plates. May Gibbs could infuse great drama into similar work, making the absence of colour immaterial, but the result with Dorothy Wall's work, however, was rather drab. *The Crystal Bowl*, ultimately, is spoilt by uneven work and an effete quality, which *Tommy Bear* had managed to avoid.

Perhaps the publishers perceived this lack of rigorous economy in Wall's early work for there were no more major commissions for more than a decade. In that intervening period she devoted herself to commercial art, the high point of which was the colour fashion covers for a Sydney magazine, *The Woman's Budget*, between 1930 and January 1932.

If it was the realistic life of the bush that had inspired Wall's most effective illustrations in *The Crystal Bowl*, then she clearly reaffirmed this interest more than a decade later in her next book, *Jacko — the Broadcasting Kookaburra*, by Brooke Nicholls (1933). This was the real life saga of a nationally famous character: it was not really a fantasy and, in fact, contained a strong educational commitment to inform children about the life and habits of the kookaburra:

Many kookaburras will not laugh in captivity. Some will only laugh at the rising and the setting of the sun. I think I am the only one that will laugh whenever I am wanted to. That is in wireless broadcasts and in record-making; and it is why I am known to so many people. [2]

'The Jackass thought that he had never seen anything so funny' by Dorothy Wall from THE CRYSTAL BOWL, Melbourne, 1921.

'He received such a thrashing ...' by Dorothy Wall from THE CRYSTAL BOWL.

And it was in this book that we first hear of Blinky Bill:

After we had played at the theatres in the city, the Doctor made us pack up and go with him all over the country. We went to Ballarat, and lots of towns in the bush. The Doctor got a native bear called Blinky Bill. He had to climb up a little gum-tree and eat leaves while I gave my laugh. [3]

Jacko was published by Angus & Robertson and marked the beginning of Dorothy Wall's association with this publishing company. The encouragement she gained from this commission and the imaginative seed planted by the name 'Blinky Bill', combined to inspire a major children's book. *Blinky Bill: The Quaint Little Australian* was both written and illustrated by Dorothy Wall and published at the end of 1933.

By the 1930s, in Australia as well as internationally, animal stories were replacing fairy stories as the most popular subject for children's books. No doubt this change in taste in Australia was partly due to public concern for the native fauna and particularly for the koala whose numbers had been severely reduced by widespread hunting in the 1920s. In the illustrative field before this time, Norman Lindsay's Bunyip Bluegum was the best known koala character in Australian children's literature. Much of the flavour of *The Magic Pudding* (1918) was provided by the antics of its three koalas, especially Bunyip Bluegum. Lindsay's koalas were individual creations; their shape, gestures and facial expressions told the whole story and they became something of a trademark for their creator.

Vignette illustration by Dorothy Wall from BLINKY BILL GROWS UP *Sydney, 1934.*

Norman's brother Lionel also realised the comic possibilities of the koala. In 1909 he started a series of full-page drawings in the *Bulletin* to advertise Cobra boot polish. The characters he drew, especially the dapper koala, delighted adults and children alike. During the First World War, a selection of this koala's exploits appeared in *The Adventures of 'Chunder Loo'.* When depicted in a slouch hat, these koalas, like May Gibbs' gumnut corps, became a symbol of Australia's fighting spirit.

However, the pictorial precedents set by Norman and Lionel Lindsay were isolated examples and belonged to an earlier generation. Dorothy Wall's character Blinky Bill was to become part of Australia's pictorial vocabulary and it is quite possible that her success was also a direct inspiration for Australia's most renowned children's book authors and illustrators, Ida Rentoul Outhwaite and May Gibbs.

It cannot be mere coincidence that 1933 was also the year in which Outhwaite introduced her most popular koala character in the comic strip 'Benjamin Bear'. She had used koalas in her earlier books and illustrations, but these were in a fairyland setting where they provided one of the few touches of Australian colour. In her comic strip they inhabited more of a realistic setting. Her koalas were always more like teddy bears than the Australian marsupial. Perhaps Winnie-the-Pooh's worldwide popularity helped renew interest in

'She saw a little man standing close beside her' by Dorothy Wall from BRIDGET AND THE BEES*, London, 1934.*

'Blinky, Splodge and Wally' by Dorothy Wall from A Tiny Story of Blinky Bill*, Sydney, c.1942. The following three illustrations, which depict the sinking of the boat, could easily be frames for an animated cartoon.*

'Blinky, Splodge and Wally' by Dorothy Wall from A Tiny Story of Blinky Bill.

'Blinky, Splodge and Wally' by Dorothy Wall from A TINY *S*TORY OF *B*LINKY *B*ILL.

Australia's own lookalike. Two years later, Outhwaite's only book devoted to koalas, *Sixpence to Spend*, was published. Was it sheer coincidence that both Dorothy Wall and Ida Rentoul Outhwaite should begin concentrating on a koala character in the early 1930s? It was to be almost another decade before May Gibbs introduced the koala as a major character into one of her own books (and that only the year after Dorothy Wall died), *Mr & Mrs Bear and Friends* (1943).

After the first Blinky Bill book appeared, a further three major titles using this character were published by Angus & Robertson as well as four minor works and a collected edition in 1939. Blinky Bill titles have remained in print ever since.

Blinky Bill has his own distinctive personality, which has endeared him to many young Australians. But what was Dorothy Wall herself like? The workaday commercial artist and mother struggling to make a living is clearly revealed at the height of her popularity in the 1930s by her letters to Angus & Robertson from her country retreat. These usually contain sad, rather pathetic, requests for loans and advances and various small favours. They convey the impression of a woman with more ambition than her talent and self-imposed isolation could achieve and a naive belief that a major career could be established without personal business skills and on-the-spot attendance.

No doubt she was often exasperated by the profile May Gibbs achieved. There were times when work by both appeared in the same magazines, although Gibbs' was always given pride of place. Wall's efforts to interest the daily press in her cartoon strips were unsuccessful, but May Gibbs' strips continued to be popular and widely syndicated. Nevertheless, Dorothy Wall did achieve one thing that constantly eluded and frustrated May Gibbs in the 1930s — a significant publication on the international scene. Dorothy Wall's *Brigid and the Bees* was published in London in 1934 and in America the following year. Unfortunately it was hardly the international breakthrough she craved and her efforts to break into the world of animation were doomed from the start. Her well-meaning intermediaries were publishers and literary agents who had little if any experience in the American world of animated cartoons.

It has been argued, with well-chosen pictorial evidence, that Dorothy Wall adapted and modified her style in the mid 1930s to make it more suitable for animation. [4] Even so, it would appear that she over-estimated her abilities in this direction: 'I know there is no one in Australia who could handle the cartoons as well as I could'. [5]

Furthermore, her rather autocratic manner in her approach to the film studios could not have helped: 'I know exactly how I would want the cartoons carried out and the smallest detail would have to be in accordance with my ideas ...'[6]

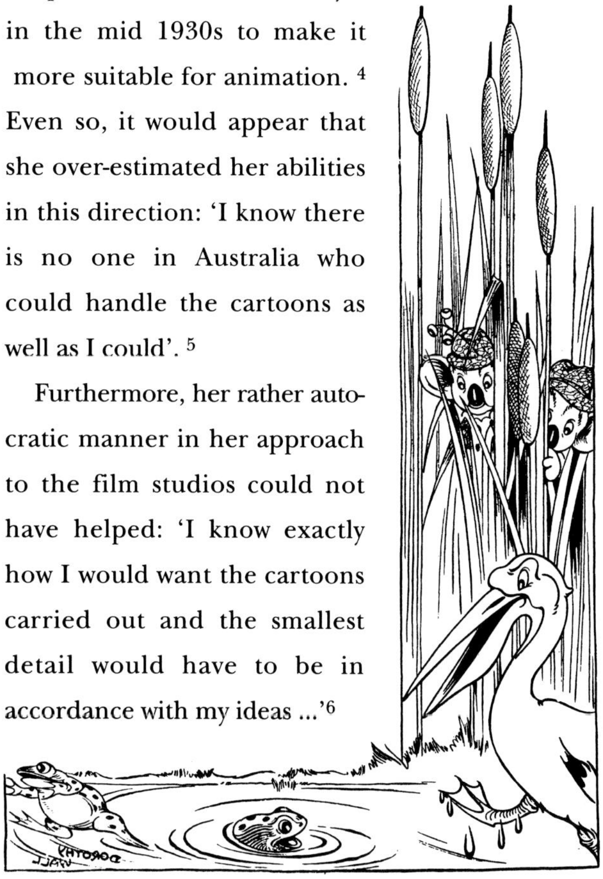

From TOMMY BEAR AND THE ZOOKIES *by Dorothy Wall, Sydney, 1920.*

BLINKY BILL
AND NUTSY
DOROTHY WALL
A
DOROTHY WALL
BOOK

If her attempts at comic strip art were any indication, Dorothy Wall did not have 'the skill of placing characters and dialogue in the correct [illustrative] relationship to make the story flow logically and sequentially'. [7]

Yet, interestingly enough, there is evidence in her works of the early 1940s, usually dismissed rather carelessly, which proves she was overcoming this lack of skill. Her illustrations for *The Tiny Story of Blinky Bill* (c.1942) show an expert grasp of the sequential skill as well as the untrammelled pictorial sense needed for cartoon work. There is clear evidence here that her style was developing and who knows just what may have been produced had she not died so unexpectedly in January 1942?

Throughout the 1930s, Dorothy Wall was the most popular and prolific newcomer and virtually the only children's book illustrator of any distinction appearing in new editions. As such her work bridges the gap between the best of Ida Rentoul Outhwaite and May Gibbs, and the later 1940s work of Peg Maltby and company.

ENDNOTES

1 'Franziska,' "An artist and her work",' *Australian Women's Mirror*, 4 December 1934, p.11.

2 Brooke Nicholls, *Jacko — The Broadcasting Kookaburra* (Sydney: Angus & Robertson, 1933), pp.10–11.

3 Ibid, p.54.

4 Walter McVitty, *Dorothy Wall the Creator of Blinky Bill* (Sydney: Angus & Robertson, 1988), Chapter 14.

5 Letter from Dorothy Wall quoted in McVitty, Op. cit., p.123.

6 Ibid, p.124.

7 Ibid, p.152.

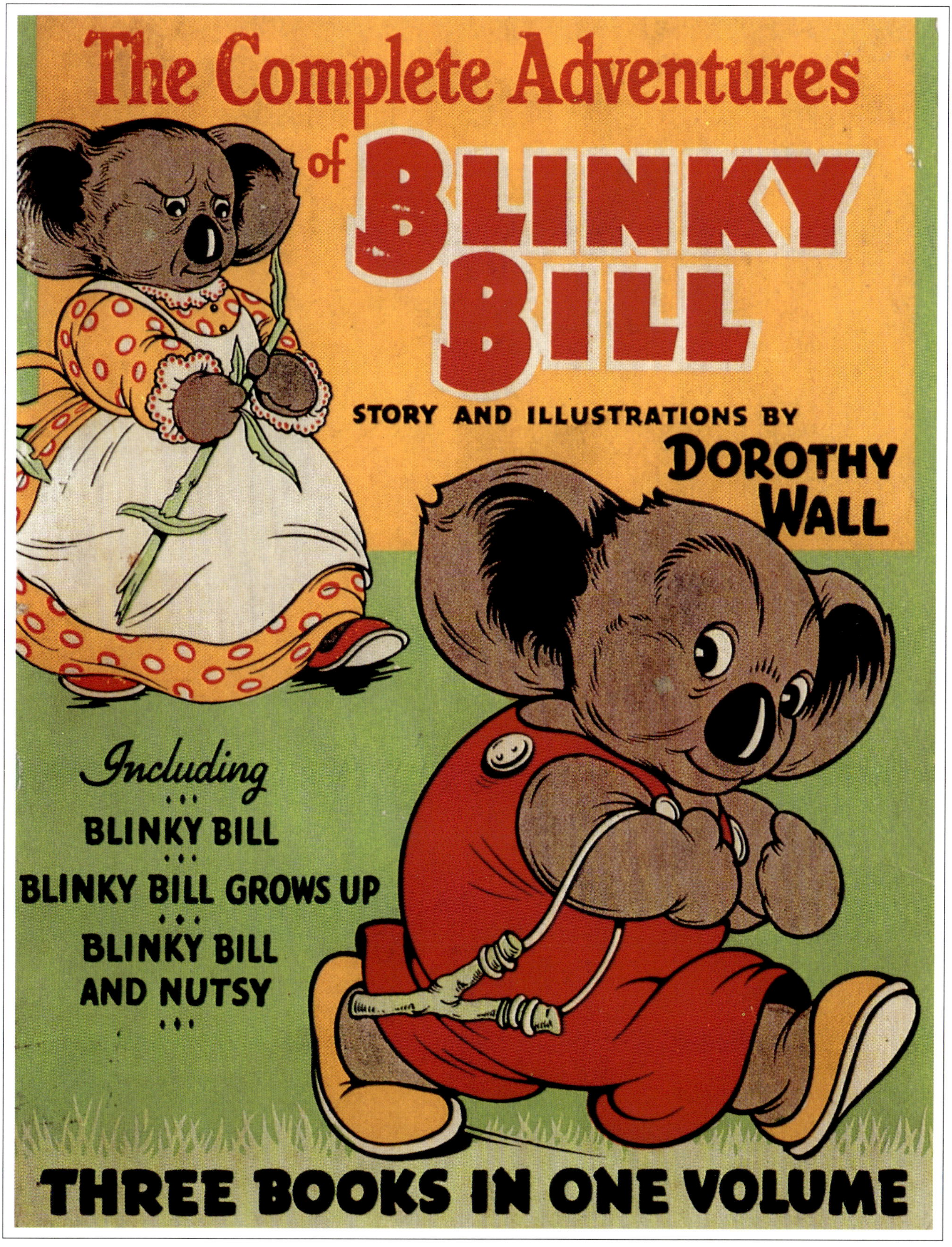

The dustjacket of the first edition of THE COMPLETE ADVENTURES OF BLINKY BILL, *Sydney, 1939.*

'Gumnut babies' by Peg Maltby. With its May Gibbs derivation, this watercolour provides a link between first and second generation fantasy illustrators.

Pixie O'Harris, Peg Maltby & Jean Elder

A Second Generation of Fantasy Illustrators

The longest running career of any Australian children's book illustrator has been that of Pixie O'Harris. Between the early 1920s and the late 1980s, she established and maintained a profile that made her almost as much a household name as May Gibbs.

Rhona O. Harris was born in Wales in 1903 and emigrated to Australia in 1920, when 16 years old. For the previous two years she had been a member of the Royal Art Society in Cardiff and although her father was a moderately successful portraitist and President of that Society she was, and remained, largely a self-taught artist. The Harris family's first landfall was Albany, Western Australia, and during their stay of less than a year O'Harris managed to contribute fantasy illustrations to an exhibition of the West Australian Society of Arts. The Governor visited this exhibition and O'Harris' autobiography records her displeasure with the artistic confusion her work aroused in the viceregal mind:

> *The Governor came and asked to meet me. He thought I had copied my drawing from the style of Ida Rentoul Outhwaite. I was rather indignant and said I'd never heard the name and that it sounded like a patent cough mixture to me.* [1]

Had she but realised it, she was being paid quite a compliment. By 1920, Ida Rentoul Outhwaite was one of the most accomplished pen and ink artists and children's book illustrators in Australia and was about to embark on a decade of international success. Outhwaite had also established a national pictorial vocabulary in Australia with her 'Elves and Fairies' style and Pixie O'Harris' work then, as now, demands comparison and evaluation within this genre.

Pixie O'Harris arrived in Australia at a time when greater talents than hers were striving unsuccessfully to find a niche in this 'Elves and Fairies' school of fantasy illustration. Outhwaite had established and dominated the market since 1903 and such figures as Ethel Jackson Morris and Ethel Spowers were either experiencing bitter disappointment, or learning to extend their talents and aspirations into alternative artistic fields, such as printmaking. What was it about Pixie O'Harris that marked her out for such artistic survival and longevity?

Most significantly, she was an ambitious, hard working and prolific illustrator whose talents were popularised on a wide front: newspaper and magazine illustrating, writing, broadcasting, mural painting, caricature and cartoon work, fashion drawing and the designing of bookplates, sheet music covers and stationery. Between 1920 and 1940, only four major works of hers were published and while they contain

Fancy Dress cartoon from the BULLETIN by Pixie O'Harris.

her best writing and illustrating it was the works thereafter that captured public attention. During the 1940s O'Harris' name was firmly established on the national scene.

She made her publishing debut with illustrations to Maud Liston's *Cinderella's Party* (Adelaide: Rigby, 1923). This book is clearly the work of a young, untrained illustrator. The unsophisticated style and weak compositions lack both the drama that pen and ink work can achieve as well as any imaginative ornamentation, which could give them decorative strength. They can only be considered in company with the first similar and tentative works by Ida Rentoul in 1903 and Ethel Jackson Morris in 1907. Two years later, *The Pixie O'Harris Fairy Book* was also published by Rigby and showed a distinct advance in compositional strengths and maturity of line.

This newfound confidence was undoubtedly the product of O'Harris' considerable exposure to the demands of newspaper and magazine illustration. *Aussie*, the *Bulletin*, the *Green Room*, the *Sydney Mail*, the *Triad*, the *Woman's Budget* and others provided a consistent marketplace for large pen and ink works, vignette illustrations, decorative lettering and humorous drawings. She had also enrolled at Julian Ashton's Art School for a brief period and taken up a position at John Sands where her illustrative talents were called upon to provide a varied range of decorative and commercial art work. O'Harris' training during this period was intense and demanding and the effect of its discipline is obvious in *The Pixie O'Harris Fairy Book*. Greater finesse and line control now show in compositions of some charm

'The beauty of the garden took her breath away' by Pixie O'Harris from PEARL PINKIE AND SEA GREENIE*, Sydney, 1935.*
After May Gibbs, this second generation fantasy illustrator was undoubtedly Australia's
best known and most prolific artist.

'Laughter' by Pixie O'Harris from THE PIXIE O'HARRIS FAIRY BOOK, *Adelaide, 1925.*

Mermaid illustration by Peg Maltby from SPEAK-WELL BOOK II*, Melbourne, 1947.*

and distinction and prove that Pixie O'Harris was taking a place as a black and white artist of note in Australia. Indeed, she could be considered the natural successor to Ruby Lindsay who had died tragically young in 1919.

For the first time we can see some evidence of O'Harris' claim that English illustrators such as Arthur Rackham and Heath and Charles Robinson were a 'wonderful source of inspiration' to her. [2] In this book as elsewhere, her vignette illustrations merit most attention and some of these overlooked pieces show a predilection for gentle grotesquerie, which her fellow English illustrators could indeed have inspired.

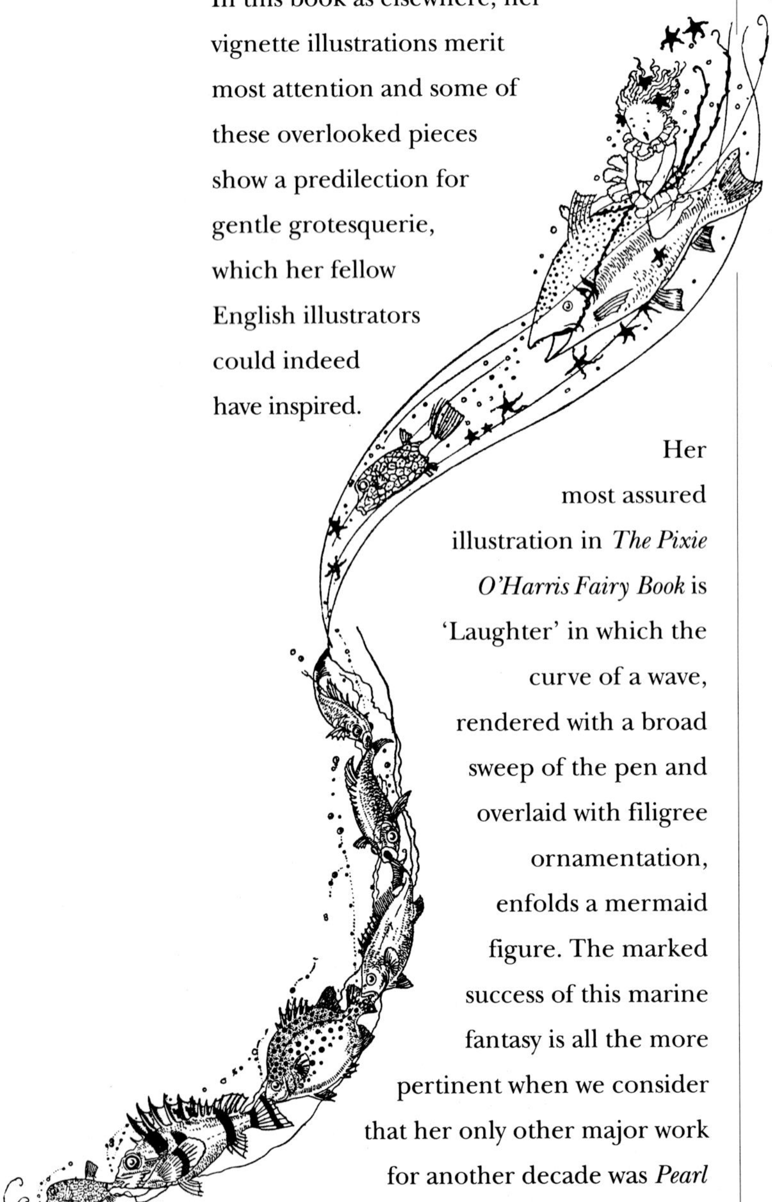

Her most assured illustration in *The Pixie O'Harris Fairy Book* is 'Laughter' in which the curve of a wave, rendered with a broad sweep of the pen and overlaid with filigree ornamentation, enfolds a mermaid figure. The marked success of this marine fantasy is all the more pertinent when we consider that her only other major work for another decade was *Pearl Pinkie and Sea Greenie* (1935). *The Pixie O'Harris Fairy Book* also shows another side to her developing talent — the figure of the author who contributed six short poems.

In the 1930s, the Depression effectively put a stop to much cultural life in Australia and illustrated children's books were certainly a luxury few publishers were willing to risk. No new titles by May Gibbs and only one by Ida Rentoul Outhwaite appeared, although reprints and comic strips kept their names before the public.

D. H. Souter died early in the decade and Dorothy Wall was the major flourishing talent.

Pixie O'Harris first solo effort, *Pearl Pinkie and Sea Greenie* (Sydney: Angus & Robertson), was published in 1935 and was markedly different from the boisterous and Australiana-based imagery of Dorothy Wall. O'Harris' gentle marine fantasy contains her most effective colour illustrations. It is certainly the most lavish children's book published by Angus & Robertson during this economically restricted decade and its four full-page colour plates make it one of the few illustrated children's books of any merit in its day. Fifteen years earlier May Gibbs had produced her own marine fantasy, *Little Obelia*. The anthropomorphic element in O'Harris' writing is certainly less well managed than in that of her forebear. However, the two rock-sprites of the book's title inhabit a miniature world vibrant with colour and incident and the illustrations are among Pixie O'Harris' best.

Throughout the 1930s, O'Harris was a regular and esteemed contributor to the *School Magazine* (NSW) and the *School*

'I will not have Cow-fish in my garden' by Pixie O'Harris from PEARL PINKIE AND SEA GREENIE.

Illustration by Pixie O'Harris from THE FAIRY WHO WOULDN'T FLY *(1947). Pixie's flower fairies are kin to those which appear in Ida Rentoul Outhwaite's* BUNCH OF WILDFLOWERS *(1933).*

'Elf and Fairies' by Pixie O'Harris from THE PIXIE O'HARRIS FAIRY BOOK.

Paper (Victoria). School and municipal libraries at this time had nowhere near the resources they possess today, and such magazines were prime reading material for young Australians. In 1940 a selection of her contributions to these ephemeral publications was issued as *The Pixie O'Harris Story Book* and reissued in an enlarged format in 1948. This second edition contained a new colour plate, 'Where is my home?', which depicts a fairy encircled by a host of grotesque elfin figures. It is arguably her most accomplished published illustration in colour and was clearly inspired by her long devotion to Arthur Rackham's work. A companion volume of further work from school magazines, *Pixie O'Harris' Gift Book,* was published in 1953.

Throughout the 1940s Pixie O'Harris' indefatigable output was further diversified by her authorship of the Poppy Treloar trilogy (1941–47) and the painting of numerous fantasy murals in children's hospital wards, baby clinics, kindergartens, day nurseries, school libraries and doctor's rooms. Her work as a community artist can be placed in context with a little-known Australian tradition that may have been inaugurated as early as 1910 in Prince Henry's Hospital (Melbourne) by Ida Rentoul Outhwaite, Edith Alsop and others.

O'Harris' work was further popularised by a series of successful exhibitions starting in 1937. Together with fellow illustrator Joyce Abbot, she first showed at the Wynyard Book Club, Sydney, in June 1937. In the 1960s she achieved a more consistent exhibition profile, which she continued until the mid-1980s. Towards the end of her life two autobiographical volumes extended her audience and appeal still further.

Pixie O'Harris belongs to the second generation of Australian fantasy illustrators: she was a newcomer to the field when

BEN AND BELLA.
AT THE BEACH.
BY
P. MALTBY.

'The First Peep' by Peg Maltby. Maltby's pictorial and imaginative debt to May Gibbs is obvious.

Outhwaite and Gibbs were at their most accomplished and her own career was not fully launched until the 1940s. Under these terms she shares a position with two other fantasy illustrators of note working in Australia at the same time, Peg Maltby and Jean Elder. The work of all three displays many of the same illustrative concerns as well as the same strengths and weaknesses. They depict a gentle fantasy world without the threat of something as primitive as a Banksia Man. While Pixie O'Harris introduced Welsh folklore elements into an Australian setting, Peg Maltby imported English woodland settings and creatures into a second generation May Gibbs world. Jean Elder sometimes added a touch of Disney-like whimsey with animated beetles, an insect orchestra and elfin figures.

While Angus & Robertson were popularising Pixie O'Harris in the 1940s, the Melbourne based publishing firm of Murfetts promoted Peg Maltby as an alternative fantasy illustrator. Murfetts' prolific output, which included work by Ida Rentoul Outhwaite, was similar to a host of low cost publications that flooded the Australian market. Similar companies published the work of Kay Druce and Connie Christie and all were distributed through toy and gift wholesalers more as stationery items than standard bookshop stock. Wartime restrictions were responsible for these cheap and standardised formats, large print runs, poor quality paper and production and the lack of a comparative overseas standard against which to measure this local output.

Peg Agnes Newberry Maltby (nee Orchard) was born in 1899 in the town of Ashby-de-la-Zouch, West Leicester, England. This quaintly named olde-worlde town and its surrounding countryside were to be combined with Peg's adopted Australian setting 30 years later as a backdrop for her fantasy illustrations. Peg's father was the local surgeon and the example he provided as an amateur watercolourist and naturalist was as formative to her as the artistic and theatrical example of Herbet and Cecilia Gibbs was to their daughter.

While May Gibbs was studying at art school in London, Peg Maltby was being introduced to the illustrative work of Arthur Rackham and Edmund Dulac. The former's *Peter Pan in Kensington Gardens* (1906) was to remain Maltby's life-long favourite, often consulted for inspiration and example. Her debt to her English upbringing and its gentle setting is especially evident in her fondness for using woodland creatures as central characters in her work.

Peg Maltby arrived in Australia in 1924 and after a brief sojourn in Western Australia (which Gibbs had left in 1913 and O'Harris in 1921) settled in Melbourne. Like Gibbs and O'Harris, Peg moved on the periphery of the Australian art world. [3] Her decorative talent was initially employed in commercial art work and then briefly subjected to the formal discipline of the National Gallery School's evening classes.

From Peg's Fairy Book by Peg Maltby, Melbourne, 1944.

'A fairy scene' by Peg Maltby from Peg's*Fairy Book, Melbourne, 1944.*

'Around the cauldron' by Peg Maltby from PEG'S FAIRY BOOK, *Melbourne, 1944.*

By the mid-1930s, Peg's illustrative debt to her Australian forebears, particularly May Gibbs, was evident and a gift of one of her watercolours to that artist elicited the following praise: 'Thank you for the lovely little picture — I think it is really sweet. The colouring beautiful, technic [sic] perfect and whole effect charming ... one with your talent should have great success.' [4]

Maltby became the most significant illustrator to utilise May Gibbs' pictorial vocabulary. In mid-1943, an exhibition of her fairy paintings at Kozminsky's Galleries in Melbourne attracted the attention of Murfetts and with a story line added to various pictures *Peg's Fairy Book* was launched the following year. Its immediate and continued popularity generated five editions that sold more than 180,000 copies and resulted in a further successful reprint in 1975. This book still commands an audience today; it certainly contains some of Maltby's best work which was described as 'carrying on the traditions of Arthur Rackham, Ida Rentoul and May Gibbs'. [5]

'Mrs Bear's Shop' by Pixie O'Harris from THE PIXIE O'HARRIS STORY BOOK, *Sydney, 1940. Pixie's pictorial and imaginative debt to May Gibbs is obvious.*

After wartime restrictions on imports were lifted, the open Australian market discouraged much of the local children's book publishing, and fantasy work was rejected for a more prosaic vision: ' ... the war stopped the taste for fairies — in parents anyhow — and the fairies fled, appalled at the atom bomb'. [6]

Maltby's last titles, apart from reprints, were produced in 1951 and include *Ben and Bella in the Gardens* whose setting in the Melbourne Botanic Gardens endeared it to many children of the day. Thereafter she turned her attention to establishing a gallery for the exhibition of her paintings at Olinda in the Dandenongs outside Melbourne. By the mid-1950s, her versatile imagination was employed in depicting more realistic characters in Australian bushland settings. Aboriginal children, rather than fairy folk, now became her prime characters and were reproduced in a wide range of prints.

Some of the inspiration for this changed pictorial emphasis was undoubtedly due to the contemporary work of Pixie O'Harris who had illustrated Frank Dalby Davidson's *Children of the Dark People*, first published in

'Where is my home' asked Wattle. 'I'm lost' by Pixie O'Harris from The Pixie O'Harris Story Book.
This is perhaps Pixie's most accomplished fantasy illustration and a homage to Arthur Rackham.

1936 and frequently reprinted. Also influential was Elizabeth Durack's work and the pottery and wall plaques of Brownie Downing, which popularised her vision of Aboriginal children before their introduction into children's books in the 1960s. More immediate credit should also be given to William Ricketts, a neighbour at Olinda, whose sculpture sanctuary was established in 1935. Ricketts' carvings and clay figures of Aborigines must also have inspired Peg Maltby's fairyland dioramas of the time which, until her husband's death in 1967, were maintained as attractions in the Olinda Gallery.

Jean Elder (b. 1915) is the third figure who made a significant contribution to fantasy children's book illustration in Australia in the 1940s. Her career actually started before Peg Maltby's, in 1937, but the war temporarily halted her efforts so that her major output, like Maltby's, was part of the immediate post-war years.

She first appeared in H. C. F. Morant's *Whirlway* (1937), which was praised for its presentation of prehistoric life in an engaging and educational format for a young audience. After the war she reappeared as an illustrator and cover artist for magazines, including the *Woman's Weekly*. With increased confidence and acclaim she provided fantasy texts as well as fantasy illustrations for more than 20 slim children's books. The most notable of these were two books written by herself and Phyllis Johnson; *Robbie's Trip to Fairyland* (1946) and *Robbie's Birthday Wish* (1950).

The original illustrations from these most productive years prompted Jean Elder's first major exhibition in 1987 and the opinion that she was 'in the same class as ... May Gibbs and Ida Rentoul Outhwaite'. [7] While this ambitious claim cannot be substantiated it is true that her work was a popular contribution to the fantasy genre during the immediate post-war years in Australia.

In style, choice of colours and subjects and in presentation, her work is sometimes very similar to that of Peg Maltby. The crowded compositions full of scurrying elfin figures, olde-worlde cottages and fairyland treats were, however, destined to have a shortlived popularity. A demand for more realistic illustration by more professionally trained illustrators in more carefully designed and presented picture books brought a whole new look to the nursery literature of young Australians.

'What a shame it is we have to go!' cried Robbie by Jean Elder from ROBBIE'S TRIP TO FAIRYLAND, *1946.*

May Gibbs based her work on a close and personal observation of the Australian bush and was motivated by a desire to foster an appreciation of our native flora and fauna. May Gibbs' plea in her first major Australian children's book was to 'be kind to all Bush Creatures'. In contrast, Pixie O'Harris, Peg Maltby and Jean Elder found their inspiration less tied to observable reality and relied on the example of illustrative forebears to a large extent. There was a lamentable dearth of second generation illustrative talent in the fantasy genre in Australia and these three were not sufficiently skilled to sustain Australia's earlier imaginative tradition. In their limited, albeit popular, hands the golden age of Australian fantasy illustration came to a gentle end.

NUTCHEN OF THE FOREST by Peg Maltby, 1945.

FAVOURITE NURSERY RHYMES by Connie Christie (c. 1950)

ENDNOTES

1 Pixie O'Harris, *Our Small Safe World* (Sydney: Boobook Publications, 1986), p.10.
2 Ibid, p. 136.
3 The only Australian children's book illustrator to achieve recognised exhibition profile remains Ida Rentoul Outhwaite.
4 Unpublished, undated letter from May Gibbs to Peg Maltby, 1930s. In Maltby family possession.
5 Harold Herbert, 'Peg Maltby's Art,' *Argus*, 25 May 1943, p.5.
6 Ida Rentoul Outhwaite, quoted in *The Fairy World of Ida Rentoul Outhwaite* by Marcie Muir & Robert Holden (Sydney: Craftsman Press, 1985), p.136.
7 Robert Gould quoted in Edmund Doogue, 'Pursuing her Muse at 72,' *Age*, 21 November 1987, p.11.

'Robbie meets the fairy cobbler' by Jean Elder from ROBBIE'S BIRTHDAY'S WISH *(1950).*

Chronology

YEAR	D. H. SOUTER	MAY GIBBS	HAROLD GAZE	IDA RENTOUL OUTHWAITE
1860–1881	**1862** Born in Scotland	**1877** Born in England		
1881–1900	**1899** *Bubbles, His Book* (London edition, 1900) **1900** *Gum Leaves*		**1885** Born in New Zealand	**1888** Born in Melbourne
1901–1910				**1904** *Mollie's Bunyip* **1906** *Mollie's Staircase* **1907** *Gum Tree Brownie* *Australian Songs for Young and Old* **1910** *Bush Songs of Australia*
1911–1920		**1912** *About Us* **1916–1918** Five booklets *Gumnut Babies* *Gum Blossom Babies* *Boronia Babies* *Flannel Flowers & Other Bush Babies* *Wattle Babies* **1918** *Snugglepot and Cuddlepie* **1920** *Little Ragged Blossom*	**1917** *If I Could Fly* **1918** *The Wicked Winkapong* **1919** 'The Mite Merry Series' *The Simple Jaggajay* *The Billibonga Bird* *The Chewg-Um Blewg-Um* *Coppertop* **1920** *Coppertop Cruises*	**1911** *Before the Lamps are Lit* **1913** *More Australian Songs for Young and Old* **1916** *Elves and Fairies* (Launched at Ida's first solo exhibition) **1920** Ida's first London exhibition
1921–1930		**1921** *Little Obelia* **1923** *Nuttybub and Nittersing* **1924** First children's comic strip commences in Sydney *Sun* *Chucklebud & Wunkydoo* **1925** *Bib and Bub, Their Adventures* 1929 *Bib and Bub, Their Adventures in Gumnut Town*	**1921** *The China Cat* *The Enchanted Fish* *War in Fairyland* **1924** *The Goblin's Glen* *Last Fairy Tales* **1925** *Tales of a Little Brown Man*	**1921** *The Enchanted Forest* **1922** *The Little Green Road to Fairyland* *The Little Fairy Sister* **1926** *Fairyland* **1928** *Blossom* **1930** *Bunny & Brownie*
1931–	**1933** *Bush Babs* **1935** D.H. Souter dies	**1940** *Complete Adventures of Snugglepot & Cuddlepie* **1941** *Scotty in Gumnut Land* **1943** *Mr and Mrs Bear* ***and friends*** **1969** May Gibbs dies	**1931** *The Wonder World Fairy Tale Book* **1962** Harold Gaze dies	**1958** Last Book, *Legends from the Outback* **1960** I.R. Outhwaite dies

Chronology

DOROTHY WALL	P. O'HARRIS, P. MALTBY & J. ELDER	OTHER PUBLICATIONS	OTHER EVENTS
		1879 *Cole's Funny Picture Book*	**1871** Edith Alsop born **1874** Lionel Lindsay born **1872** Ethel Turner born **1878** Mary Grant Bruce born **1879** Norman Lindsay born
1894 Born in New Zealand	**1899** Peg Maltby born in England	**1894** *Seven Little Australians* by Ethel Turner 1897 *Teens* by Louise Mack 1890 *Dot & the Kangaroo* by Ethel Pedley	**1885** Ruby Lindsay born **1886** Ruby Winckler born **1890** Ethel Spowers born **1891** E.J. Morris born **1895** Christian Yandell born Olive Crane born **1898** Ethel Pedley dies
	1903 Pixie O'Harris born in Wales **1915** Jean Elder born	**1905** *The Little Black Princess* **1908** *We of the Never Never* **1910** *A Little Bush Maid* (first Mary Grant Bruce book) *Some Children's Songs* illus. by E. Alsop *Bushland Stories* illus. by L. Lindsay	**1901** Margaret Clark born **1907** First Australian Exhibition of Women's Work **1909** First 'Chunder Loo' by Lionel Lindsay appears in the *Bulletin* **1910** Walter Cunningham born Children's Ward, Homeopathic Hospital, Melbourne, decorated by Outhwaite, Alsop & others
1920 *Tommy Bear & the Zookies*		**1916** *The Cobweb Ladder* illus. by E. Alsop *Adventures of Chunder Loo* illus. by L. Lindsay **1917** *Australian Nursery Rimes* illus. by N. Lindsay, D.H. Souter, etc **1918** *The Magic Pudding* illus. by N. Lindsay **1920** *A New Book of Old Rhymes* illus. by B. MacDonald	**1916** Elizabeth Durack born **1919** Ruby Lindsay dies
1921 *The Crystal Bowl*	**1923** Pixie O'Harris' *Cinderella's Party* **1924** Peg Maltby arrives in Australia **1925** *Pixie O'Harris Fairy Book*	**1921** *The White Butterfly* illus. by E.J. Morris 'Us Fellers' comic strip by J.C. Bancks *Arrows of Longing* illus. by E. Spowers *A Book for Kids* by C.J. Dennis **1925** *Australian Fairy Tales* illus. C. Yandell **1928** *Judy and Punch* (last Ethel Turner book)	**1924** Brownie Downing born Walter Cunningham arrives in Australia
1933 *Blinky Bill* *Jacko* **1934** *The Amazing Adventures of Billy Penguin* *The Tale of Bridget & the Bees* (American edition, 1935) *Blinky Bill Grows Up* **1935** *Brownie* **1936** *Stout Fellows* **1937** *Blinky Bill & Nutsy* **1939** *Complete Adventures of Blinky Bill* **1940** *Blinky Bill Joins the Army* **1942** Dorothy Wall dies	**1935** Pixie Harris' *Pearl Pinkie & Sea Greenie* **1939** Pixie O'Harris first begins painting murals **1940** *Pixie O'Harris Story Book* **1942** Pixie O'Harris' *Marmaduke the Possum* **1942** Pixie O'Harris' *The Fairy Who Wouldn't Fly* **1944** *Peg's Fairy Book* illus. by Peg Maltby **1946** Jean Elder's *Robbie's Trip to Fairyland* **1950** Jean Elder's *Robbie's Birthday Wish* **1991** Pixie O'Harris dies	**1932** *The Fairies Tree* illus. by M. Wood **1936** *The Flyaway Highway* by N. Lindsay *The Magic Pudding* (first American edition) **1941** *The Way of the Whirlwind* illus. by E. Durack **1942** *Billabong Riders* (last Mary Grant Bruce book) **1946** *Dusty* by Frank Dalby Davidson	**1946** Childrens' Book Council inaugural Awards **1947** Ethel Spowers dies **1952** J.C. Bancks dies **1956** Christian Yandell dies **1958** Edith Alsop dies **1961** Lionel Lindsay dies

Bibliography

BOOKS AND CATALOGUES

Anderson, Hugh, *The Singing Roads: A Guide to Australian Children's Authors and Illustrators,* Parts I & II, Wentworth Press, Sydney, 1965, 1969.

Barton, Charlotte, *A Mother's Offering to her Children,* 'Gazette' Office, Sydney, pr., 1841.

Chaplin, Harry , *Norman Lindsay: His books, manuscripts and autograph letters,* Wentworth Press, Sydney, 1969.

Chaplin, Harry, *A Lindsay Miscellany,* Wentworth Press, Sydney, 1978.

Clark, Margaret, *Fairies: being original drawings by Margaret Clark,* Sweetacres, Sydney, c. 1918.

Eisenberg, Joseph, *Olive Crane 1896 [sic]–1935* [Exhibition Catalogue] N.E.R.A.M. Armidale, NSW, 1987.

Hetherington, John, *Norman Lindsay: The Embattled Olympian,* O.U.P., Melbourne, 1973.

Holden, Robert, *Cheer Up Children* [Exhibition Catalogue], Prince Henry's Hospital, Melbourne, 1986.

Holden, Robert, *May Gibbs and her Fantasy World* [Exhibition Catalogue], James Hardie Industries Limited, Sydney, 1984.

Holden, Robert, *The Plague of Lindsays* [Exhibition Catalogue], National Trust, Sydney, 1986.

Holden, Robert, *Souter's Cats,* Angus & Robertson, Sydney, 1988.

Holden, Robert & Andrew Mackenzie, *Snugglepot and Cuddlepie and Other Fairy Folk of the Australian Bush* [Exhibition Catalogue], National Herbarium, Sydney, 1987.

Jose, Arthur W., *The Romantic Nineties,* Angus & Robertson, Sydney, 1933.

Lindsay, Daryl, *The Leafy Tree: My Family,* Cheshire, Melbourne, 1965.

Lindsay, Rose, *Model Wife,* Ure Smith, Sydney, 1967.

Lindsay, Norman, *Letters of Norman Lindsay,* Angus & Robertson, Sydney, 1979.

McVitty, Walter, *Dorothy Wall the Creator of Blinky Bill,* Angus & Robertson, Sydney, 1988.

Moore, William, *The Story of Australian Art,* 2 vols. Angus & Robertson, Sydney, 1934.

Muir, Marcie, *A Bibliography of Australian Children's Books,* 2 vols., Andre Deutsch, London, 1970, 1976.

Muir, Marcie, *A History of Australian Children's Book Illustration,* O.U.P., Melbourne, 1982.

Muir, Marcie & Robert Holden, *The Fairy World of Ida Rentoul Outhwaite,* Craftsman Press, Sydney, 1985.

O'Harris, Pixie, *Our small safe world,* Boobook Publications, Sydney, 1986.

Polya, Rosemary, *Australian School Science Text-Books, 1850–1939: A Bibliography,* La Trobe University, Victoria, 1986.

Richards, Michael, *People, print and paper* [Exhibition Catalogue], National Library of Australia, Canberra, 1988.

Sorenson, Edward S., *Life in the Austalian Backblocks,* Whitcombe & Tombs, London, 1911.

Thomas, Daniel (ed.), *Creating Australia,* Art Gallery South Australia, Adelaide, 1988.

Walsh, Maureen, *May Gibbs Mother of the Gumnuts: Her Life and Work,* Angus & Robertson, Sydney, 1985.

ARTICLES & NEWSPAPER REVIEWS

'Art Exhibitions ...' *Argus,* 22 June 1920, p.7

'Art Exhibitions: Miss [sic] Outhwaite's Pictures', *Sydney Morning Herald,* 25 July 1928, p.17

'Art Exhibitions ...' *Sydney Morning Herald,* 1 June 1926, p.10

'Art Notes ...' *Age,* 4 August 1925, p.9

'Art Notes ...' *Age,* 2 August 1927, p.7

'Australian Art & Artists', *Building*, August 1915, p.128

'The Bulletin Zoo', *Bulletin*, 10 December 1908, Red Page

Colquhoun, A. 'Victorian Art ...' *Herald*, 23 September 1916, p.16

Colquhoun, A. 'Victorian Artists ...' *Herald*, 9 May 1916, p.1

Colquhoun, A. 'Water Colour & Pen Work ...' *Herald*, 7 November 1921, p.7

Coppel, Stephen 'Claude Flight and his Australian Pupils', *Print Quarterly*, v.2 no.4, December 1985, pp.263–283

['Ethel Spowers'] *Women's World'*, September 1927, p.493

'Franziska', 'An Artist and her work', *The Australian Women's Mirror*, 4 December 1934, pp.

Herbert, Harold 'Peg Maltby's Art', *Argus*, 25 May 1943, p.5

Hervey, Grant 'Black-and-white-Australia', *Steele Rudd's Magazine*, v.3 no. 9, October 1906, pp.802–817

Holden, Robert 'The Olive Crane Exhibition', *Insight*, no.1 April 1987, pp.9–11

MacNally, J. 'Fairy Drawings': Miss Margaret Clark's Work', *Daily Telegraph*, 18 August 1926, p.12

McVitty, Walter 'Pixie O'Harris — Writer and Illustrator', *Reading Time*, no.58, January 1976, pp.4–8

['Margaret Clark'] *Sydney Morning Herald*, 18 August 1926, p.11

Marlowe, Mary 'Mother of the gum nut babies: May Gibbs at home', *Women's World*, 1 December 1922, p.13

['May Gibbs'] *Womens World*, 1 December 1922, p.13

Mills, Carol 'Ruby Lind: The little known Lindsay', *This Australia*, v.3 no.3, Winter 1984, pp.80–86

Moore, William 'Careers for Australasian Girls. IX — What the artist's life offers', *New Idea*, v.6 no.13, December 1907, pp.848–849

Moore, William 'D.H.S., A prodigious worker', *Sydney Morning Herald*, 5 October 1935, p.13

'One day she feels about 100, but mostly she's 12', *Sydney Morning Herald*, Women's Section, 12 November 1953, p.4

Outhwaite, Ida Rentoul 'Lesson 34: Developing the Imagination', Art Training Institute, Melbourne, 1947

Outhwaite, Ida Rentoul 'The Troubles of an Australian Illustrator' *Age* Literary Section, 21 January 1939, p.9

'Percy Lindsay, Artist', *Lone Hand*, June 1919, p.12

'Queen of the Gum-Nuts: Bush Lore Portrayed — May Gibbs at work', *Sunday Sun*, 11 March 1917, p.14

[Review of Ida Rentoul Outhwaite's *Elves & Fairies*] *Bulletin*, 4 January 1917, Red Page

B, J.L.G. [John Le Gay Brereton] [Review of Norman Lindsay's *The Magic Pudding*] *Hermes* v.24 (new series) no.3, November 1918, p.318

'Ruby Lindsay', *Herald*, 18 March, 1919

Schell, Frederick B. 'How Books are Illustrated', *Centennial Magazine*, v.1 no.2, September 1888, pp.118–121

'Sisters in art and letters', *Australian Book Buyer*, v.1 no.9, December 1912, p.221

'Society of Artists' Exhibition', *Sydney Mail*, 14 September 1921, p.39.

Stow, Randolph, 'Our Children in Cole Lane', *Australian Letters*, v.1 no.3, April 1958, pp.14–22

['Art Reviews'] *Sydney Mail*, 19 January 1921; 14 September 1921

'The Sydney Pictures', *Herald*, 5 November 1907, p.2

W. N.E. 'New Doulton Ware: Australian art and English Craftsmen', *Art & Architecture*, v.3 no.4, 1906, p.157

'Women's Page', *Sydney Mail*, 19 January 1921, p.16

MISCELLANEOUS

Lothian Papers, State Library of Victoria.

Taped Interview with Pixie O'Harris by Hazel de Berg, National Library of Australia, Tape 366, 16 April 1969.

Original Illustrations

Locating the original artworks for Australian children's illustrated books of the past can be a frustrating and disappointing exercise. All too often this work has not survived, or has been overlooked or even disparaged by collectors and institutions. The Museum of Australian Childhood has provided some of the most notable originals in A GOLDEN AGE from its developing collection. Its holdings of published and unpublished artwork span the last 90 years of Australian history and offer an unparalleled representation of the best in Australian children's book illustration. I am also indebted to the following people who allowed me access to treasured originals: Margaret Standfield (nee Clark), the Hon. Ashley Dawson-Damer, Janet Fraser, Josef Lebovic, Kay and James Overton, Tom Quirk and Dr and Mrs Neil Shand.

All originals illustrations are works on paper with dimensions given in centimetres, height preceding width.

PAGE 17: 'Scared of the Kewpies' by Ola Cohn. Pen and ink and watercolour, 41.5 x 27.5, 1914. Private collection.

PAGE 18: 'Jilted' by D.H. Souter. Pen and ink, brush and ink, 32 x 24, 1933. Josef Lebovic Collection.

PAGE 36: 'The Secret Pool' by Ida Rentoul Outhwaite. Pen and ink and watercolour, 45.6 x 27.2, 1920s. Museum of Australian Childhood Collection.

PAGE 46: 'Five O'Clock Tea' by Ida Rentoul Outhwaite. (Published as 'Mr. Merman and his Daughter' in *The Little Fairy Sister*, 1923. Pen and ink, 36 x 27.5, c.1922. Private Collection.

PAGE 49: 'Flower Frocks' by Ida Rentoul Outhwaite from *The Enchanted Forest*, 1921. Pen and ink, 37 x 28.5, c.1920. Museum of Australian Childhood Collection.

PAGE 54: 'My Little Son Dandelion' by Ethel Jackson Morris from *The White Butterfly*, 1920. Pen and ink, 378 x 28.5, c.1919. Museum of Australian Childhood Collection.

PAGE 56: Vignette illustration by Ethel Jackson Morris from *The White Butterfly*, 1920. Pen and ink, 17.2 x 12.5, 1920. Museum of Australian Childhood Collection.

PAGE 57: Vignette illustrations by Ethel Jackson Morris from *The White Butterfly*, 1920. (top) Pen and ink, 13.8 x 11.7, c.1920. (bottom) Pen and ink, 17.1 x 12, 1920. Museum of Australian Childhood Collection.

PAGE 58: 'An Old Woman' by Ethel Jackson Morris from *The White Butterfly*, 1920. Pen and ink, 19.5 x 14, 1916. Museum of Australian Childhood Collection.

PAGE 59: Vignette illustration by Ethel Jackson Morris from *The White Butterfly*, 1920. Pen and ink, 14.3 x 10.5 (sheet size), 1915. Museum of Australian Childhood Collection.

PAGE 60: Vignette illustration by Ethel Jackson Morris from *The White Butterfly*, 1920. Pen and ink, 14.2 x 20 (sheet size), c.1916. Museum of Australian Childhood Collection.

PAGE 61: 'Came dancing towards her, two Beautiful Fairies' by Ethel Jackson Morris from *The White Butterfly*, 1920. Pen and ink and watercolour, 37.5 x 26.4, 1919. Museum of Australian Childhood Collection.

PAGE 64: 'Children on a Flying Horse' by Ethel Spowers. Pen and ink, 25 x 27.5, 1926. Private Collection.

PAGE 66: 'Children in a Tree' by Ethel Spowers. Pen and ink and watercolour, 25 x 7.5, 1927. Private Collection.

Page 67: 'Card playing by moonlight' by Ethel Spowers. Pen and ink, 18 x 25.8, 1920s. Private Collection.

PAGE 68: 'The Witch Dance' by Ethel Jackson Morris from *The White Butterfly*, 1920. Pen and ink, 18 x 12, 1915. Museum of Australian Childhood Collection.

PAGE 70: 'The Noisy Parrot' by Ethel Spowers. Colour linocut, 24.8 x 21.7, 1926. Private Collection.

PAGE 74: 'Mary, Mary, Quite Contrary' by Ida Rentoul Outhwaite. Watercolour and pencil, 82.5 x 107, 1910. Prince Henry's Hospital Collection.
'This is the Way we Wash our Hands' by Edith Alsop. Ink and watercolour, 82.5 x 108.3, 1910. Prince Henry's Hospital Collection.

PAGE 78: 'The Witch and the Giant' by Christian Yandell from *The Gates of Dawn*, 1977. Pen and ink, 20.5 x 15, 1930s. Museum of Australian Childhood Collection.

PAGE 83: 'The Foundling Fairy' by Harold Gaze. Pen and ink and watercolour, 33.5 x 24, 1921. Museum of Australian Childhood Collection.

PAGE 97: Colour lithographic poster by May Gibbs for the Department of Public Health (NSW), 73 x 48, 1920. Museum of Australian Childhood Collection.

PAGE 107: 'The Boat Race' by May Gibbs from *Nuttybub and Nittersing*, 1923. Pen and ink and watercolour, 24.5 x 19, c.1922. Private Collection.

PAGE 121: 'The Florist Shop' by Margaret Clark. Pen and ink and watercolour, 30.5 x 20, 1920s. Museum of Australian Childhood Collection.

PAGE 122: 'The Spirit of Mischief' by Margaret Clark. Pen and ink and watercolour, 30.5 x 20, 1920s. Museum of Australian Childhood Collection.

PAGE 132: 'Chunder Loo bike riding' by Lionel Lindsay from *The Adventures of Chunder Loo*, 1916. Pen and ink and charcoal, 40.5 x 31.5. Private Collection.

PAGE 135: 'The March Past' by Percy Lindsay from *The Magic Billabong*, 1928. Pen and ink, 19 x 15 , c.1927. National Trust (NSW) Collection.

PAGE 137: 'The Lamplighter came down the street' by Ruby Lindsay from *Naughty Sophia*, 1912. Pen and ink, 33 x 22.5 (mount size), c.1911. Museum of Australian Childhood Collection.

PAGE 138: 'Old Father Time' by Ruby Lindsay. Unidentified magazine illustration. Pen and ink, 24.5 x 30.5, c.1912. Museum of Australian Childhood Collection.

PAGE 162: 'Gumnut Babies' by Peg Maltby. Pen and ink and watercolour, 25.8 x 16, 1940s. Museum of Australian Childhood Collection.

PAGE 164: Fancy Dress Cartoon by Pixie O'Harris for the *Bulletin*. Pen and ink, 31 x 24.5 (sheet size), 1925. Museum of Australian Childhood Collection.

PAGE 166: 'Laughter' by Pixie O'Harris from *The Pixie O'Harris Fairy Book*, 1925. Pen and ink, 31 x 24.5 (sheet size), c.1924. Museum of Australian Childhood Collection.

PAGE 179: 'Where is my home' asked Wattle. 'I'm lost' by Pixie O'Harris from *The Pixie O'Harris Story Book*, 1948. Pen and ink and watercolour, 27.6 x 21.8, c.1947. Private Collection.

Index

Book titles are listed in the body of the index and also appear as subheadings under author's name; illustrations are listed as subheadings under booktitles, or as subheadings under illustrators if they did not appear in books. Page numbers for illustrations are in ITALICS.